BETWEEN TRAINS

BETWEEN TRAINS

Barry Callaghan

McArthur & Company

Toronto

First published in Canada in 2007 by
McArthur & Company
322 King St. West, Suite 402
Toronto, ON
M5V1J2
www.mcarthur-co.com

Library and Archives Canada Cataloguing in Publication

Callaghan, Barry, 1937-
     Between trains : stories / Barry Callaghan.

ISBN 978-1-55278-631-4

     I. Title.

PS8555.A49B48 2007   C813'.54   C2007-900228-5

Cover design by Tania Craan
Interior by Michael P. M. Callaghan
Printed in Canada by Friesens

The publisher would like to acknowledge the financial support of the Gov-
ernment of Canada through the Book Publishing Industry Development
Program (BPIDP) and the Canada Council for our publishing activities.
The publisher further wishes to acknowledge the financial support of the
Ontario Arts Council for our publishing program.

10 9 8 7 6 5 4 3 2

To those nighttime talks
with D. in the
winter of 2006

and as always
Crazy Jane Claire.

The modern world is not evil; in some ways the modern world is far too good. It is full of wild and wasted virtues. When a religious scheme is shattered ... it is not merely the vices that are let loose. The vices are, indeed, let loose, and they wander and do damage. But the virtues are let loose also; and the virtues wander more wildly, and the virtues do more terrible damage. The modern world is full of the old Christian virtues gone mad.

— *G.K. Chesterton*

CONTENTS

BETWEEN TRAINS

It was a small train station. I sat in the stifling stillness of the waiting room, staring at junk food vending machines until the storyteller came in and sat down and offered me a drink from his silver flask. "Bourbon," he said, "Knob Creek," leaning back in his chair, waiting for me to say something about whatever it was I had on my mind about stories, because that's what he had agreed to come down from his house in the hills to talk about after I had called him up, telling him, "I'm between trains."

I didn't say anything, I watched the old man's eyes, and I guess it looked like I was wondering whether I could trust him, but it wasn't that – I was wondering if he trusted me on first meeting, so I said, to relieve him of any idea that he was going to end up under obligation to me, "I've got no story to tell you or for you to look at to read. I was just hoping to hear something from you."

He leaned forward, smiling in a confiding kind of way, and said, "You just sit still, because I always thought the best storytelling, in case you were going to ask, is still as still water."

I looked him in the eye, pondering, and wondering if I should get myself a soda from one of the vending machines, but instead I said, "I don't know any stories like that," and I reached for his whisky flask.

"Trust me" he said, as I took a swallow of whisky.

A moment or two passed, and then, as if he had been testing the silence, and he had decided that it had become our silence, he said, "This is a story I'm going to tell you that's about a real death, and how anything that's really real in the past – like a death – keeps coming at you out of the future, and this story happened at the racetrack where there was this young trainer who was wanting to ingratiate himself with an old trainer – and the young fellow said – because he knew that there'd been a death in the family – 'I hear your brother died,' and the old trainer says, 'Yes, that's right.' And the young trainer asks him, 'And how long has he been dead?' So the old trainer says, close up to his ear, 'If he'd lived till Saturday he'd be dead a year.'"

He looked me in the eye and I looked him in his eye.

"Is that a story?" I asked.

"Sure it is."

"If that's a story then I really am between trains."

"We're all between trains," the old man said, "but if that won't do, then I'll tell you what another writer once told me in Paris when I was about your age. He told me how he was talking to a small group of school girls and he told those girls that any good story, when you get right down to it, is all about brevity, religion, mystery, sex, aristocracy and plain language – and so, sure enough one of those girls wrote him a story for when they met the next day and the story she wrote went, 'My God,' said the Duchess, 'I'm pregnant. I wonder who did it?'"

He held up his hands as if he were under arrest. This stopped me from either laughing or complaining and then he closed his eyes and sat back in his station house chair. I took another drink of whisky. The storyteller and I sat as still as still waters could be.

FIRST COMMUNION

My first communion was in late March or early April. There was wet snow on the ground. I was six years old and I was walking alone to church – my mother had dressed me in a grey suit and a celluloid collar with a big white silk bow. An older boy on a bicycle, a delivery boy, was riding toward me. I had a snowball in my hand. When the delivery boy was about thirty feet away, lost in myself and not giving it a thought, I made a behind-the-back flip of the snowball – as if, by throwing it from behind my back, the delivery boy would not know who had thrown it. As a throw of perfect timing in a perfect arc it caught the delivery boy on the chest – he rode right into it. The astonished boy got off his bike. I stood in my little grey suit, amused at myself. The boy didn't seem angry, he seemed bewildered, knowing that he had to do something, so he punched me in the chest, knocking me to the seat of my pants in the wet snow. It never occurred to me to fight back – I had done something reckless, and anyway I was too small. All I can remember was sitting in a church pew, my celluloid collar scraping my neck, the seat of my flannel pants muddy and wet, but I was full of wonder – not because I had thrown a snowball at a bigger boy but wonder at the looping curve of the ball in its flight, my knowing as soon as I'd let the snowball go that it was going to hit home, knowing that the only reason the delivery boy was there riding on the street was to end up caught in the falling arc of light. The punch, the dirty wet pants, were inconsequential; I'd been so entranced by the sight of my perfect snowball that I can't remember taking my First Communion.

PIANO PLAY

Al Rosenzweig was called Piano by his friends. He agreed to meet with me to eat a smoked meat sandwich at Switzer's Deli. Piano was a big man who appeared affable because he was slow moving and because of his ample pink cheeks and jowls. I knew he was a killer. The police knew he was a killer. They couldn't prove it but they knew that after the Maggadino family from Buffalo had tried to kill Maxie Baker outside the Towne Tavern so that the mob could take over the gambling that was controlled in Toronto by the Jews, Al had driven to Niagara Falls and had strangled two of Maggadino's men with piano wire. But he was not known as Piano because of the wire. It was because he played the piano at a Bathurst Street high-rise social club for survivors of Shoah every Thursday night, where he liked to sing Irving Berlin and Cole Porter songs:

> *Let's do it,*
> *let's fall in love*

As I arrived at the table Piano was singing to himself.

He looked up and said, "Take a pew with a Jew."

We ate our smoked meat sandwiches, and then I said to him, "Piano, I know business is business but we both know Solly Climans for a long time. He's a good guy."

"So he's a good guy. I even knew his father, Fat, I booked his father's bets, too, but he owes money, too much money."

"I'm worried about him."

"Why worry? If he pays, he's good."

"He's beyond scared, Piano, he says he's gonna commit suicide."

"He ain't gonna commit suicide."

"I believe him."

"You believe him?"

"Yeah, I believe him."

"Jews don't kill themselves."

"Believe me, he's gonna kill himself."

Piano wiped his lips with his napkin.

Drumming his fingers on the table, he began to hum *birds do it, bees do it*, and then he said, reaching out to touch my hand, "Jews don't kill themselves. They sometimes kill each other but, believe you me, they don't kill themselves."

He shrugged, as if I should have known we were helpless before a truth, a truth that allowed him his amiable consideration for me.

"Do yourself a favour," he said, "try a little dessert, a cheesecake, it'll look good on you."

DAPHNIS
AND CHLOË

Susanne and Anna-Marie were young professors at the university, Susanne an anthropologist and Anna-Marie a linguist.

After attending an evening performance of Górecki's *Third Symphony* at the Beach's Bandshell, they were sharing a glass of Bordeaux, Chateau Longueville, to celebrate the joy they felt even though the music had been so painfully sad.

The phone rang.

Susanne went to answer it and when she came back she was quietly laughing to herself.

"What's the joke?"

"It was a student of mine. She knew she shouldn't call me so late, but she's upset by a conversation we had about her father in my office this afternoon. I think she's in love with me."

"Oh no."

"We were talking about men, actually about our fathers, and whether as men they had done us harm. She said her father had really hurt her – I think she meant he had molested her. And when she asked about my father I told her the truth. I told her that when I was a child, 'Okay,' my father would say, 'I'll wash you down as far as possible and I'll wash you up as far as possible, and you wash your possible yourself.' She didn't laugh and instead touched my wrist and asked if she could kiss me. I said, 'Anything is possible except that,' and she seemed very hurt, like I wasn't taking her seriously."

"Students are so demanding these days," Anna-Marie said.

"So, tonight on the phone she wanted to know if I could tell her how evil had come into the world. And I told her that Aquinas and Augustine had taken a crack at that and we're none the wiser, nobody's sure."

"I guess that wasn't what she wanted to hear."

"I suppose not."

"No."

"My goodness, evil of all things."

"Yes, well, it's late. Let's go to bed and be evil so we can make love."

They went into their bedroom, turned off the light and got undressed in the dark, sure of themselves in that light.

A PROMISE OF RAIN

Officers of the Ice Palace died during the war: Sedelnikov, Chulpenyev, Belov. Names. Ice on the tongue, silver bells in the mouth, that's what the poet Tsvetayeva said – *A name, click of a gun, deep sleep.*

Grandmother, at 101, shrivelled to the size of a little girl's crib, called for her brother, our great-uncle Victor, who had lost a leg at Stalingrad, clean cut above the knee.

He kept it encased in a lead box in the family crypt, afloat in embalming oils. A respected lexicographer, he visited his leg once a year, lit a candle, said a prayer, and flaunted his affairs with young soldiers in the lobby of Hotel Astoria.

He died despised in an S & M whipping stall at a military punishment club. Even so, he was a compassionate man who talked to us about evil, how the tear in a needle's eye comes from laughter, and how men like Stalin, Himmler, Beria, not only know the evil they do but find it wryly amusing in all its intricacies of device, the way pulling the wings off butterflies is ferociously funny to queerly strung choir boys.

What else could their defiant sign WORK MAKES FREE over the gate of a death camp be but a joke that only killers could enjoy? They knew, they knew, they knew, and they laughed, he said, as they laughed at work, work, the dignity of work in the work camps of Siberia.

What a joke, which is how he thought of his leg, a length of space filled with phantom flex, a twitch, an ache, resurrected in those stalls, as he took the lash so that he could lie down in laughter at the pain of inexplicable, baseless hatred, silver bells in his mouth, ice on his tongue, names: Sedelnikov, Chulpenyev, Belov.

DREI ALTER KOCKERS
(THREE OLD FOGIES)

1

ZOL GOT, HORUKH HU, MIKH
HITN FAR PAYN UN SHMARTSEN

*May God, blessed be He, protect
me from anguish and pain*

• Yiddish prayer, said over the challah every Sabbath •

Herschel Soibel, born in the Jewish quarter of Lublin and brought up on the Street of Furriers, was from a pious family prominent among Hasidim in the trade for fur hats.

At Herschel's *bris*, when the rebbe cut his penis the women were astounded to hear him let out a long sigh.

His father rejoiced, saying he had heard in his son's sigh the call of the *tzaddic*, he had heard Ezekiel, the righteous man: "He shall reap the fruit of his own righteousness . . . ."

At the age of three Herschel could read and write, by four he could cross-stitch, and at eight, he sat at a small desk on the weekends where he read Torah. Using a porcelain inkwell, he wrote up bills of sale for heavily bearded men dressed in long greasy gabardines, men who spat into their palms before clasping hands on the price of a *shtreimel*, a broad-brimmed hat made from the tails of seven sables. Herschel handed any man leaving the shop a card that had printed on one side: *Beware of the Wisdom of Fools . . . In Our Hearts We Know Our Hats,* and printed on the other side: EZEKIEL 18:20

❀   ❀   ❀

In 1943, the Soibel family of nine, among the last Jews alive in the Lublin wartime ghetto, were driven out of their apartment by men with riding crops and bayonets and herded through the streets into cattle cars. They were transported to Auschwitz.

❀   ❀   ❀

Each Soibel packed and carried a small suitcase or a satchel; in Herschel's suitcase, a silver menorah, and in his father's satchel, silver Shabbat candlesticks. Paper money was sewn into the lining of dresses and suitcoats.

"Wherever we're going we'll negotiate," Herschel's father said, "among the *goyim* there's always a price."

The train came to a halt in the night, the cattle-car doors were unsealed, and an SS officer strode up the ramp to the doors, crying, "*Aussteigen.*"

Stupefied men, women, youths and children stumbled down the ramp under floodlamps to be met by two thin SS officers who said, "*Gut gemacht,* here are the men who will help you," pointing to Jews wearing prisoners' stripes. They belonged to a labour crew that was called Kanada by other prisoners in the camp because Kanada was a dream-country and to work in this crew meant that the men not only got their loaves of bread, but fresh kosher sausage – and also, they received a daily ration of vodka. From time to time they were allowed an uneasy sleep – five or ten minutes – in the grass on the embankment beside the train tracks.

The Kanada crew had to haul the dead from the cars to trucks; then they stripped the living and pushed and bullied the infirm who were naked and naked mothers who were delirious, the addled naked and the naked young, and the naked elders into line-ups on to the road that led from the ramp to the crematorium, yelling, "You'll have a shower, you'll see, you'll feel better."

After the arrivals had been cleared away, the crew portioned-off all the bread, the marmalade, the meats, and pickled herring they could empty out of broken-open satchels and suitcases. The few men, women, and youngsters who had been cordoned off to the right of the condemned, those Jews selected to live, were sent to the barbers from Zauna who were waiting to shave their heads. They were deloused and given their stripes. Most of the jewels, the rings, the bracelets and broaches, the gold watches ripped out of the piles of clothing, were handed over to officers who filched gold for themselves and sent the rest to Berlin to be melted down to help pay for the war.

After the clearing of the ramp, several of the Kanada crew stretched out under the shade of old chestnut trees that lined the last stretch of rail track up to the camp, and one of the well-fed crew asked, with sudden concern, "What'll we do if they suddenly run out of Jews, if the trains stop coming?"

❉   ❉   ❉

Herschel's family was fed into the ovens in the camp, his mother, father, and four girls on the first night, and over the months, his two brothers were burned in the ovens, too.

One day at dusk, Herschel saw, in the play of falling light, the face of an angel in the smoke rising from the stacks – he was sure it was Ezekiel's angel, the avenger – but then the face turned to ash.

He asked an elder, a gaunt rebbe: "If the angels have gone up in smoke, has not God, too?"

The rebbe, without looking at him, said: "*A mensch tracht, un Got lacht.*" [1]

*　　*　　*

In 1945, on a cold winter's morning, as Soviet armoured divisions crossed the Vistula river and advanced into Poland, the prisoners in the camp were rousted out of their bunks and barracks and driven onto backwoods roads to begin a long death march west, into Germany.

Herschel, losing several toes to frostbite, survived the march.

Outside Bratislava, after the Nazi surrender, he celebrated his *bar mitzvah* birthday in the back of a GI troop truck. The GIs were black. One gave him a bottle of Coca Cola. A rebbe blessed him and said, "God is good."

Herschel said, "Beware of the wisdom of fools."

"I am not a fool," the rebbe said angrily, "and neither is God."

---

[1] A man makes plans, and God laughs.

"And so why," Herschel demanded, "are the Nazis not dead in their iniquity? Why are we, in our righteousness, dead, like my papa, like my mama, dead?"

❉   ❉   ❉

In a squalid displaced-persons camp outside Vienna, Herschel told a Red Cross nurse something an old prisoner had told him: "There are three truths: – One, you can only trust life itself by believing lies – 'Have a shower, you'll feel better;' – and, two, just as profoundly absent as the presence of God is the absence of privacy – 'If you are sleeping six starving men to a bunk, never mind the lice, the leg cramps, the snoring, it is the shit . . . these men shat all over themselves and each other in the night. And just as they never say God's name, they never speak of this shit'; – and finally, shoes, a man with no shoes is a man who has no future."

Herschel told this to a Jewish Red Cross nurse after she had tried to stroke his arm.

"I don't want to be touched," he said. "Nothing frightens me, only human kindness makes me afraid, may *Hashem* forgive me."

He drifted out of the displaced-persons camp and went to Vienna where he worked for a fence as a runner, carrying gold to be melted down. "Behind everything there is always an oven," he said.

He became a small-time fence himself.

He let it be known: for Herschel, a deal was a deal, a contract a contract. He was unforgiving. He cut the cheek of a young *shvindler* who cheated him.

"You're a hard man," a buyer from Prague told him.

"I'm only fourteen."

"Even so, you're a hard man."

"I wish."

❉   ❉   ❉

In Toronto, he worked as a masseuse-boy and towel attendant at the Grange public steam baths, and then as an apprentice to Nathan the Fish Monger in the Kensington Jewish market, becoming expert in beheading and deboning huge carp. He stood the fish heads on a rack behind him, the eyes staring, accusing. At seventeen, Herschel, working during the day for Morris Fisch, a furrier on Spadina Avenue, enrolled in night classes at Harbord Collegiate where the other students were nearly all the sons of refugee Ukrainians. For generations, Jews had owned farm lands in Ukraine and one young man's family had worked on a Jewish farm. He called Herschel a "Kike." Herschel spent two nights in jail and was expelled from the school for chopping off the Ukrainian's little finger with a deboning knife.

"I wanted to put his finger up with the fish heads."

"Such a scandal is what Jews don't need," Morris Fisch said. He was the owner of Cadillac Furs, Tri-bells, a semi-pro basketball team, and a contributor to the mayor's re-election campaign. He threatened, over coffee with the Mayor's assistant, that if charges were not dropped, he would publicly name several local Ukrainians as *Kapos*, black shirts, and war criminals, but he also offered to send Herschel to Israel to work on a kibbutz.

"For you to make *aliyah*," he told Herschel, "to live in the Holy Land, this could be everything."

"It could also be nothing," Herschel told Fisch. "They don't wear hats in Israel. It's too hot. They wear stupid caps. Me, I'm from a family of hatters."

He showed Fisch a *Toronto Star* photograph of a hockey crowd in the lobby of Maple Leaf Gardens, and said, "Look, a thousand men all wearing hats, fedoras. For the money you'd waste on me in Israel, make me a loan instead for a shop."

"You're going to sell *shtreimel*?"

"In Lublin, we were pious hatters. Here, I will be a stylish hatter."

"And I," Fisch said, laughing, "am Alice in Wonderland."

Herschel, who had no idea in the world who Alice was, told him what Ezekiel said, "*Ki lo echpotz bemos hamis neum Hashem Adonai vehashivu vichu.*" [1]

Fisch didn't understand Hebrew, so he said, "What's that mean?"

"It means, 'Get a new life.'"

※　　※　　※

He changed his name to Sable of Harry Sable Hats and opened a small store on Spadina Avenue. After a photograph of the Tri-bell basketball team players wearing pearl-gray fedoras with a black band appeared in the evening newspapers, Morris Fisch and several furriers, sports writers, hockey players, gonzos and gangsters, became his customers. When, after some three years, the young Catholic bishop — Emmett Carter — who had a reputation for elegance, let it be known in an interview in the *Catholic Register* that he'd bought a black fedora at Harry Sable Hats on Spadina Avenue, parish priests began, of an afternoon, to drop into the shop. Through the years, he sold hats to skaters in the Ice Capades, to Sammy Davis Jr. when he played the

---

[1] For I desire not the death of him that dieth, saith the Lord God, return ye and live.

Barclay Hotel, and to Sammy Luftspring, the boxer who had become a bouncer at the Brown Derby tavern, to Joe Kroll, the Argonaut quarterback, to Maxie Baker, the gambler, and to Al Rosenzweig, bookmaker, a *far-brecher* [1] enforcer for loan sharks and the Jewish mob. "I once took a finger myself," Harry told Al. Harry had met Al at the Victory Burlesque theatre, next door to his hat shop, when both had gone to see the Miss Sepia Top Hat Colored Girls Review "direct from Chicago." Harry had said to Al, "There are two ways you can tell about a man. Look at his woman, look at his hat. The woman who's on top is in his bed, the man he wants to be is on his head."

Harry and Al became abiding friends, sometimes sharing a Cuban cigar in a smoking room Harry had outfitted for clients above the shop, or they'd meet at Switzer's across the road from the shop for chicken soup with matzo balls, a smoked meat sandwich, and then a strudel or a cheesecake. They discovered they shared not just an enthusiasm for hand-rolled cigars but for Frank Sinatra and Peggy Lee, especially songs by Irving Berlin. Once a month, telephoning from the upstairs smoking room, they hired expensive call girls and listened to Sinatra and Lee on Harry's collection of

---

[1] A criminal.

33 ⅓, vinyl long-playing records, and they drank schnapps.

Harry's other indulgence, which he did not share with Al, was shoes. "The future is mine," he would say, happily confessing that there was something perverse he didn't want to know about himself, a man missing half his toes due to frostbite who wanted to own hundreds of pairs of shoes. "I don't go nowhere but I look good doing it." He often shopped for shoes with baseball players. "Ball players like hats and they like shoes. On the other hand, jazz musicians, they don't care what's on their feet. It's a thing you can notice."

Over the decades, Harry did not move from Spadina Avenue and he did not renovate his shop.

"Who needs to? Me is me. I'm a fixture. My shop is me, I can change where I live but not my shop. People believe they know me, they do know me," and he would point to a sign in Gothic script over the door: *Beware of the Wisdom of Fools . . . Harry Knows His Hats.*

Surprising himself in his sixties, he married a young Jewish widow he'd met on a gambling junket to Puerto Rico. After two weeks of being married, he'd asked her why she wore false eyelashes even to breakfast and she'd accused him of being barbaric because he refused to stop wearing a hat at breakfast. "That's only for *alter kockers*," she'd yelled. Once a week, of an afternoon, she went to a tanning salon. "All the time, even in December, she was brown as a nut." The marriage lasted six months. "She was too much sunlight," he told Al, "the sunlight got in my eyes. I come from the dark forests. Anyway, sometimes a loss is a gain."

As his later years went by, Harry, though successful and secure, had fewer customers. Not many men wanted to wear hats.

Very few men wore fedoras.

"Looking back, it was Jack Kennedy who did it to us," he said to Al, nodding sagely. "Everything was out in the open, bravado, the big bareheaded smile, so what happens? Kennedy, he's wearing no hat, so he gets shot in the head . . . ."

Harry settled into semi-retirement. He took a spacious two-bedroom apartment on north Bathurst Street in a 14-floor concrete slab high-rise (which was really 13, he pointed out to Al, because there was no 13th floor). All the tenants were Jewish: Shoah survivors like himself, ultra-orthodox Hasidim ("hard core," he called them), disaffected Israelis, and Jews who'd abandoned South Africa. "I'm in little Tel Aviv," he said, "which may or may not be a blessing, but where else should an *alter kocker* be?"

His only difficulty was in resettling his parrot. The parrot, a big bird of intense red and green feathers and a bold head, whose cage and perch were in the second bedroom, had been a gift – after Harry's marriage had failed – from Humberto Escobar, the Puerto Rican third baseman for the Blue Jays. For five years, Humberto had bought Harry Sable hats for himself and for his brothers and cousins in San Juan. The parrot, called Humbo in honour of the third baseman, had lived with Harry for seven years in their duplex flat in the old Annex area. Harry had come to feel enormous affection for the bird. They would sit in the stillness of an hour – at times watching eye to eye – and in these moments of enigmatic silence, Harry had taught Humbo how to say the names of concentrations camps, and the numbers of their track lines – and the squawking of those names gave Harry the only leave for laughter that he'd ever felt in his life about death. On several afternoons, since teaching Humbo the names, he had tried to explain to Al what it was like to see in his memory's eye a rigid SS officer, immaculate in black, and to hear him squawk *Auschwitz, Auschwitz,* but Al said he didn't need to know any more about the SS than he already knew, and what he knew was from the movies. He too thought hearing the parrot was hilarious, and so once a week Harry and Al would go for a walk with Humbo on Harry's shoulder, and sometimes on Al's shoulder, too.

"Humbo's one happy bird," Harry would say.

The parrot, however, did not like the high-rise elevators. He became aggressive and even abusive in the elevators, repeating the names of the camps over and over again,

Auschwitz, track 29.

Belsen, track 16.

Treblinka, track 9.

Dachau, track 3.

Humbo unnerved and outraged many of Harry's new neighbours.

Harry was riding the elevator up with Humbo. A fat man with slack jowls and very dark, almost black, eyes was riding with them. Harry, out of the corner of his eye, thought there was something familiar about the man, and though he couldn't immediately place him he was sure that they had met. Perhaps it was the hat. He was wearing a Harry Sable.

"Nice hat," Harry said dryly.

"Thanks."

"*Dachau, track 3*," the bird called.

"Quiet," Harry said.

"*Belsen, track 16*."

"Someone might wanta kill that bird," the fat man said.

"Do I know you?" Harry asked.

"*Auschwitz, track 29*," Humbo cried.

2

Jakov Przepiorko, born before the war in Warsaw, was a street orphan. "Born with soot in his hair," a policeman said, "*bist a draykop*."[1] When asked where he came from, the boy replied, "Out of town." An old rebbe, known not only in the schools but on the street as an expert on Hebrew grammar and as a mathematician, took him by the arm and asked as they walked toward the cemetery, "Which town?"

"I won't tell you," Jakov said, "so you can't send me back."

"Back?" the old rebbe said, tilting his *shtreimel* forward. "You don't fool me, your mother was a dirty brothel whore in Krochmalna Square."

"Children have been swapped," Jakov said,

"Maybe Abel for Cain. *Es regnet – Gott segnet*."[2]

The old rebbe, who came from a family of *shtetl* horse traders, got him a job tending the horses of several Jewish droshky drivers. Jakov fed, he watered, he

---

[1] A spiv, a con man.

[2] It rains, God blesses.

brushed the manes of the horses, and cleaned the pus, caused by coal smoke from household-stove fires, out of the horses' eyes.

He also had to oil down and keep pliable the drivers' leather whips.

After a month at this work, sleeping on a straw pallet close by the horses so he could steal their body heat, Jakov – following the precise instructions of the rebbe – presented the drivers with a detailed bill. He asked for his money. The drivers rolled the bill up in a ball and refused to pay him.

"Complain what you want. Tell the rebbe, we'll whip the shit out of you."

He shuffled his feet and backed away from the stalls, the drivers wagging their whip handles at him. He was grinning and they thought he must be weak-minded – but he was grinning because he had, on every day of the month – been stealing money from them, stealing from the iron cash box they kept hidden behind the heavy harnesses hanging on the wall of the stable. He had stolen two groschen pieces a day.

During the month, using the stolen money, he had also begun to lend money, going into Hasidic *yeshivas*, into the quarter around Krochmalna Street – the street of *gonifs, shvindlers* and hoodlums – demanding interest of 25 percent, one groschen to four.

At the age of fifteen, he was in business, carrying a black book, a ledger, that contained a careful listing of the names of his debtors.

Over glasses of tea he told the rebbe about the droshky drivers and he told him about his black book. The rebbe sat down, drawing his long gabardine around his ankles, and said, "Let me tell you about a precious gift we Jews gave to royalty, royalty all over Europe, it's about mathematics, this gift for money you have, since for you, how to add and subtract is something easy. It was not always so easy, not for us, not for the *goyim*. Unbelievable it may be now to our eyes, but a thousand years ago when we and the Christians did such calculations as those you are doing in your book, they were written in Latin and Hebrew. You can imagine maybe how it was to keep ledgers, to keep count let alone compound interest by Latin numbers. Impossible," and reaching for Jakov's black book he turned to a blank page and wrote:

$$\begin{array}{r} XXIV \\ -IX \\ \hline XV \end{array}$$

"Who could conduct business in such clumsiness? Also, it was Christians, not Jews, who were forbidden to travel from place to place. We Jews were free, free to go one day, free to be expelled the next day, and we took from the Arabs their numerals and added to them our *galgal*, our little *wheel*, the decimal point, that allows us to do columns of figures. We became the accountants, the keepers of compound interest and prosperity, we were hated by the Christian traders but treasured by all the great barons and royalty in their courts. No matter the hatred now, do not forget that your gift for money that makes you money is a blessing unto the Jews, a blessing still," and he laid his hand on the cloth cap covering Jakov's head.

"I, too," Jakov said, "should wear a fur hat, not a *shtreimel*, but a sable hat."

❊   ❊   ❊

Jakov saw:

A Death's Head mounted on a stake at a ghetto gate.

Tanks, flame-throwers, and machine guns.

And behind the gauleiters and the guns, in the city proper, gutted apartment houses like giant ruined and blackened molars.

For five years, Jakov – like most Jews in the Warsaw ghetto – had narrowed his shoulders and narrowed his eyes, constricted in his daily business. But he had done well. "I am no fool," he said. "I know how they dream. They intend to kill us all."

At twenty, he was tall, muscular and agile – very quick on his feet – and brazen: he was curt, crisp, and a successful *bonditt*: "I hold one hand out, my fist is in my pocket."

In 1943, as the uprsing in the ghetto against the Nazis collapsed, as tanks blew out whole apartment floors, as soldiers went door to door with flame-throwers, as they gunned down folks on the run, as the Nazis razed the ghetto, making it into a deathscape, Jakov escaped down into the underground, nearly suffocating as he inched forward through the sewage, the stench of slop and shit, at last getting out of the city into the woods. Once he was in the woods, however, entranced by the stillness and distracted by the twittering of birds, he was clubbed unconscious by a partisan who wanted his shoes, a partisan who stripped him naked and tied him up and left him in the grass for the Nazis.

❉ ❉ ❉

In Auschwitz, Jakov was ordered to work with a Kanada section crew, the "blue" commando of Jewish prisoners who were in charge of herding Jews out of the cattle cars. He worked diligently. He was then moved to the "red" section – where he helped to undress Jews who, on final inspection, had been selected to walk naked on "the road to heaven." In his mind's eye, he could not help himself, he calculated the day-to-day number of naked bodies – an arithmetic that enraged him, but then on waking each day, he was relieved to be alive, and with increasing anger he willed himself to work beyond his exhaustion. An SS officer recognized this consuming rage to live in Jakov and promoted him to the *Platzjuden,* those who were in charge of a sorting area, a kind of flea market for gabardine coats, violins, artificial legs, corsets, menstrual rags, irons and ironing boards, and shortly after that he was given a stool among the *Goldjuden,* prisoners who cleaned and sorted gold teeth that had been pried from the jaws of the dead. Finally, he became one of several *Kapos* working under a Jewish "commandant." Few prisoners were surprised that he was made a *Kapo.* Everyone, Jews and Nazis, felt in him a cold implacable fury, a fury far deeper than anger. And even more unnerving to other prisoners, he seemed to have a faith in that fury – a faith that it was his fury, if only he could keep it constant, that would carry him through from day to day, it was his fury that would keep him alive. When he heard another *Kapo* say, "We will all die, we are dead men on vacation in a life that has no meaning, no God," Jakov said: "If God created the world and created us in His own image, then this place is either proof that He is a complete failure, or this is His place, too, and there is a way to stay alive here on His terms. I do not intend to die, so I assume God is not dead."

❊   ❊   ❊

Once a month, between trains, as several of the Kanada crew stretched out on the grass under the chestnut trees and drank watery coffee and vodka, an SS officer, to amuse himself, allowed – under very close guard – two prisoners to play Russian roulette with a Colt .45 the officer had taken from the body of a dead American soldier outside the town of Casino in Italy.

A prisoner who played and came out of the game of roulette alive was given two bottles of vodka on top of his regular ration, and two days off with no work, with nothing to do but drink.

The men who chose to play roulette were usually in a state of exhausted hysteria, feverish in their sleeplessness, or, they had become "Muslimmen" – men who were apathetic and yearning to die, or, they were hopelessly drunk.

Jakov had played the game three times, sitting cross-legged in front of fellow prisoners, three men who had blown their brains out, the last of his three games played on the evening before the camp was rousted out at dawn with all the prisoners being driven from the camp to begin a forced march double-file on back roads into Germany as the Soviet armoured divisions and infantry advanced out of the east.

Several *Kapos* were strangled in the night by the marchers, but not Jakov, who – remembering how the partisan had snuck up on him in the Warsaw woods – kept close watch on everyone.

Between two snowbound villages, Jakov Przepiorko and Herschel Soibel had trudged through the snow side-by-side. They had hardly looked at each other but Herschel had said, "You're a plump little rat."

Jakov, saying nothing, had fallen back in the line.

✻   ✻   ✻

In Toronto, Jakov Przepiorko became Jake Piorko. For more than a year, with a fake driver's licence that he'd paid for with a gold tooth, he drove a half-ton delivery truck for Future Chicken, a slaughterhouse on Spadina Avenue. He was the only Jew on the trucks. The other drivers were black. Within weeks, he was running a card game in a locker room behind the Future Chicken killing floor. When one of the drivers said to him, "You ever smell anything like this joint, man?" he only smiled.

He began to lend money at high rates to the drivers who had lost at cards, and then he made a loan to a butcher who worked on the floor. "Don't make me draw blood," Jake said, trying for a small joke as he gave the butcher, whose apron was splattered with blood, the money.

"You want blood I'll show you where the blood is," the butcher said, and he took Jake to the Prince George Hotel whose owners had connections to Meyer Lansky in Havana. In the hotel, a weekly high-stakes poker game was dealt by a man with long waxen fingers, Harvey 'The Heeb' Laxor, who, seeing Jake's camp numbers tattooed on his arm, said, "No explanation necessary," and introduced him to Maxie Baker. "Mr. Piorko," The Heeb said, "meet a gambler."

"We Jews," Maxie Baker said, "we bookies, we run all the heavy games in town, we cover the horses, the whole kit-and-kaboodle from which we intend to keep out the Maggadino connection, you'll find out who they are, the *lokshen*[1] Mafia we don't have nothing to do with since a Jew always looks out for a Jew."

"As it should be," Jake said.

---

[1] Noodle

"And so, that's what's with me, I'm telling you, and so what's with you? You're from the camps, you were there?"

"It's a fact."

      ❋   ❋   ❋

Jake never spoke again about Auschwitz. With help from Maxie, he set himself up as a business man whose business happened to be loan sharking. In time, except when he had to go down lanes or into back rooms because his clients looked dishevelled and disreputable, he conducted his business from comfortable booths in three fashionable downtown restaurant watering holes: the Silver Rail, the Savarin, and Bigliardi's. Uptown, he had lobster once a week in the House of Chan, and then he went over his black ledgers with meticulous care, bringing all interest on debts to the decimal point, licking the tip of his 4H pencil, a habit he had picked up from his old rebbe in Warsaw.

For almost a year, he ponied up protection money to cops on the vice squad at 52 Station, paying them off over lunch at Sai Woo on Dundas Street, and because Maxie had shown him a section in the income tax code that referred to "all bribes, under-the-table payoffs, and illicit gambling income" as taxable, he paid his income taxes religiously, every April 15.

"They're no different than us," Maxie said, "it's all business, the government, all they want is the *vigorish*, their percentage of the take." Jake took his percentage and, identifying himself as a professional gambler who accounted meticulously for his expenses – especially his "entertainment" of the police and his forest-green Mercedes – he assumed the air of a grim, well-fed taxpayer who was in the good graces of his government. He allowed himself only a wry smile when he told his bank manager, who wanted to know (because the police would want to know) where all the cash was coming from, "I, too, lend money." The manager had said, "Thank God you're not laundering drug money," but had then apologized because Jake had looked offended. "I got a knack for making bankers feel stupid," he later told a hooker who asked him what he did for a living. "As for living, that's what I do at all cost."

Working out of fine restaurants, taking a compulsive pleasure in eating foods deep fried or cooked in butter, and having a love of wine and vodka, too, he grew jowly and plump, and then fat, weighing some 290 pounds, and he soon became known among gamblers as Fat Jake Piorko.

He gave cash in an envelope to the United Jewish Appeal, as did other mobsters, but he did not go to temple and he never let his photograph be taken, not even when Lou Jacetta, his clothier on Yonge Street, asked him if he would like a memento snapshot of himself with Bill Cosby, the comedian, another Lou Jacetta customer who flew in regularly from Philadelphia to have Jacetta make him a suit. Jakov said 'No' with such a surprising burst of anger that Jacetta said, "Jesus, you sound like you'd like to hurt me."

"No, no," he said, "sorry, but my hurting days are behind me." He left the tailoring shop and never went back.

On four occasions, however, he had had to hire Al Rosenzweig – the Piano man – to hurt four men, to collect bad debts.

"We understand each other," he'd said to Al.

"Yes. Business is business."

"A loss can be a gain," he'd said.

"Give or take a knee," Al had said, smiling.

❧   ❧   ❧

Over the years, Jake lived alone in six or seven two-and-three-bedroom apartments. In each, Jake had painted all the walls and woodwork white, and one or two of the rooms had always stood empty, with no furniture at all. Standing in those stark empty rooms, he always felt a peace he could find nowhere else.

On occasions when a delivery boy or a hooker had got into his rooms and had seen how he had surrounded himself with next to nothing, and the boy or the hooker had then said, "Wow, what a way to live!" he had cancelled his rental agreement and moved. He didn't ask himself why, he only knew that he had suddenly been overcome by an anxiety – a question, What a way to Live? – a ringing of numbers over and over in his ear, a tumbling of numbers – 27,609 – his exact calculation, his camp calculation of the naked dead he had seen walking "on the road to heaven." His anxiety only went away when he had closed the door and secured the deadlock on a new apartment.

A marriage late in life, a marriage of six weeks when he was fifty-nine, had failed, a marriage to one of his hookers. She was twenty-six and he'd been seeing her for two years. To his surprise, evening after evening, he had found her young plump nakedness strangely moving, a nakedness almost too painful, too pink, too soft, too pliable and he would stare at her as if she were a discovery, as if, in her youth, something was being reborn in him. When they made love, she made him forget how fat he was. He had given her all the money that she wanted and they had married at City Hall, but six weeks later, astonished at how intimate and easy she was, he had tried to *cum* in her from behind, and she'd said, "No, no. Not the dirt-track road. That's a private road. That's for my boyfriend." He said, "You mean you're still seeing him?" and when she said "Yes" with a shrug he hadn't tried to hurt her; he had been enraged but he had also been surprised at her guilelessness, and so did not want to hurt her. He had just told her to get out. When asked by the apartment superintendent where his wife had gone, he said, "She was good till she went bad," and he moved to another apartment.

Having gone into semi-retirement, he'd taken an apartment on north Bathurst Street. He'd grown weary, he was tired, deeply worn out, not so much in his bones but he felt his tiredness was somehow in his heart. He was eating only one meal a day, and he'd lost weight, some sixty pounds.

One morning, looking in the mirror, he said, in angry distress, "Sixty pounds, that's the weight of a six-year-old boy."

He slammed the mirror, cracking the glass.

3

Enraged, Harry was weeping, he was almost incoherent as he explained to Al Rosenzweig that someone had broken into his apartment – "Which was easy enough, since, among Jews, I didn't think I'd need a deadbolt lock – but that someone, they took nothing, they wanted nothing but to hurt me, they killed Humbo, they beheaded my parrot. The fuckers, the goddam fuckers, I can't believe it, the goddam fucking Nazi shit chopped off his head . . . ."

Al looked around for the body of the bird, or the head. *Does a bird like that bleed?* He didn't see any blood.

"No, no, never mind," Harry said, "I know who did it. Son-of-a-bitch, I knew I recognized him in the elevator, the fat shit, that bag of suet, that *schmuck*, he hated the bird . . . ."

"Who?"

"Upstairs. The fuck, he lives one floor up, he should have been killed years ago, a goddam *Kapo*, he knew I'd know once I saw him, and he was wearing one of my goddam hats, can you believe it, he's standing there under one of my hats, and he says to me in the elevator looking me right in the eye, 'Someone should kill that bird,' and he fucking-well did . . . I fucking know in my bones . . . .'"

"Maybe you know," Al said, trying to establish a calm, "maybe you don't."

"I know. Believe you me, I know."

"You I believe, but even so, maybe you're wrong. You gotta be careful about who you got in mind."

"Piorko, Jake Piorko, maybe him you know already, somehow he's heavy into the rackets."

"Piorko I know,"

"What d'you know?"

"I done business with him, he's a shark, all his life he loans money to losers, all kinds of losers . . . ."

"You two've done business?"

"A taste here, a taste there. Nothing big."

"I'll give you big, I'll tell you what I want, not just as a friend, you being my friend, but a business proposition. Kill the fuck."

"Harry, I'm older, I'm not so strong, cut it out."

"Cut out his fucking heart, I say. This isn't just me Harry talking to you 'cause he killed my bird, be-headed him, *chop chop*, like they did in the camps, this is Herschel. This is Herschel from the old world, before, when you didn't know me and you didn't know what it was like, I wouldn't want you to know, except now, so that you understand, to watch a Jew eat the bread of a Jew, to watch a Jew take the hand of a Jew and lead him to the ovens, he deserves to die."

"He's already gonna die, he's too old to live. He must be ninety-fucking-years old."

"I want *you* to kill him. I want my old pal Piano to wire him."

"No, no, this we don't talk about like pals, you and me. This is business."

"I'm talking business. It's a contract. I'm a businessman, you're a businessman. Ten thousand . . . ."

"Ten thousand what?"

"Ten thousand bucks. To kill him."

"A bird. You want I should kill Fat Jake over a bird. I can take a finger, you want to really hurt him, OK, two fingers, but it offends me, you gotta understand, it cheapens me, this is a bird," and Al stomped his foot. "This is like less than *treyf*, [1] you want me to kill a man for a bird that even someone starving would not eat?"

"Naw, for ten thousand."

---

[1] Unclean. "Every animal that has a split hoof not completely divided or that does not chew the cud is unclean for you; whoever touches the carcass of any of them will be unclean." LEVITICUS 11:26

"You think maybe because you know I wired a couple of guys that I don't take life seriously? Believe me, I take it serious, life. I'm alive, make no mistake."

"I'm serious. If the bird's not good enough for us to do the deal, so kill him for all the Jews . . . he was as ruthless as they got, a Jew cruel to Jews, to help the Nazis, he gave death to Jews and what does he do the second time when I meet him in the elevator . . . ."

"You meet him twice . . . ?"

"I saw it in his face, the first time, but I forgot till I remembered the next day who he was, my plump little *Kapo* inside that fat fuck and I tell him, 'I know you,' and then the bird starts screaming, 'Dachau, track 6, Auschwitz, track 29, I know you,' saying 'I know you' like I just said it to him, and Piorko goes nuts and grabs the bird by the throat, trying to strangle my bird, except I got Piorko by his throat, telling him, 'You fucking *Kapo*, how come you're not dead?' He should be dead."

"Maybe so, but no one did."

"No one did what?"

"Killed him. No one cared enough to kill him and now you do. I got two *alter kockers* trying to strangle each other in the elevator . . . ."

"He was trying to strangle Humbo dead but, instead, he chopped off his head."

"And so now where is the bird?"

"At the vet's."

"They're gonna put back his head, or what?"

"Cremate him. Put him in a jar."

"Cremate?"

"Yeah, for me to keep. An urn. What else have I got to keep? Twenty-five hats? Two hundred shoes? Bullshit. You kill him. Forget the bird. Like Ezekiel said, 'He that hath spoiled by violence, he that hath given forth upon usury: shall he then live? He shall not live, he shall surely die, his blood be upon him.' I make the price. Ten thousand. Cheap at the cost for all the Jews."

❧   ❧   ❧

On the third Thursday evening of every month, if he was free from business obligations, Al Rosenzweig was found playing the piano for an hour at the Bialik North Bathurst Street Social Club for Ladies and Gentlemen. He played at a white baby grand Yamaha piano, gift of the Junior Ladies Auxiliary, in a long, somewhat narrow recreation room on the "penthouse floor" of a Senior Citizen apartment house. The rec room had a small bar and parquet dance floor, several easy chairs, styled in blue or white leather (the colours of Israel), and ten or twelve card tables with four chairs at each table.

Marvin Rosenzweig, Al's father, had retired to this high-rise house but after six months he died of a heart attack. Al had been told "in confidence" by a horse-faced woman wearing a *shetle*, a wig, that his father had "broken his broken-down heart" while "doing sex" with her closest friend, an eighty-year-old widow, "once a slut always a slut," a story that both astonished and pleased Al. "What a fucking way to go," he'd said. "Exactly," the old woman had replied, slapping her wrist coquettishly.

When asked by the officious manager of the apartments what his father, who had emigrated from Berlin in the thirties, had done for a living, Al said, "Newspapers, he moved from the *Star* to the *Telegram* to the *Globe*." It was Al's own joke because his father and his mother – who had come together in a marriage arranged by a rebbe in Berlin – had, for forty years, sold newspapers from inside a small wooden, forest-green newsstand at the corner of the King and Bay Streets banking district. His father had also scalped theatre tickets, and hockey and baseball tickets. It had been a very lucrative sideline. "He had his window on the world," Al would say, "so he met a lot of interesting people. You know what he said about Fred Astaire? He said Astaire was so good he could give dancing at the end of a rope a good name."

Al amused himself by letting slip what appeared to be little confidences, especially amused if – like the Astaire story – these confidences were not true. He didn't believe inquiring strangers like the apartment manager deserved the truth; he believed men and women did what they had to do and then faced the truth. "It's like we said when we were kids: you show me yours and I'll show you mine. You learn, pecker to pecker, that what you got is what I've got, no matter." When he was asked by the manager how he had learned to play the piano, he said, "I was taught by myself to play by ear, like I play my life. Later, I was taught about music by an Irish choirmaster."

"A Catholic?"

"Yeah."

"And where was this, may I ask?"

"A church at Bloor and Bathurst, St. Peter's, on the kitty-corner to Honest Ed's Emporium and Bargain Store."

"Ed Mirvish I know. His wife collects glass eyes. From Catholic I know zilch."

"Don't worry about it."

"What's to worry? I'm too old anyway to worry, Catholics already they gave me grief."

"Me also," Al said, "I got a little grief from them myself."

"And you were born where?"

"Palmerston Avenue."

"Palmerston! So you were born here, so there you are. You play the piano. For me, this is enough."

"I don't carry none of that camp baggage," Al said.

"You're a Jew?"

"I'm a Jew but I'm not Jewish."

"This I don't understand," the manager said.

"Neither do I. That's the point. I just do what I do, I play the piano, Jewish can look after itself."

❊   ❊   ❊

The choirmaster at St. Peter's church, Harry O'Grady, had taught Al how to read music and, as a gift, had given him *The Songbook of Negro Spirituals*, which Harry liked to sing, and standing together at the piano, arm in arm, they would shout out,

> *Ezekiel saw a wheel a-rolling*
> *Way in the middle of the Lord*
> *A wheel within a wheel-a-rolling*
> *Way in the middle of the Lord*
> *And the little wheel run by faith*
> *And the big wheel run by the grace of God.*

Al and Harry had met because, as a youngster, Al had played floor hockey in the winter in St. Peter's basement with his friends from the streets around the church. "Nobody plays floor hockey anymore, it was a great church basement game. You had a sawed-off broomstick and this heavy felt disc with a hole in it . . . and if you lost the game you could beat up the other team with your broomstick."

Al learned several spirituals from his songbook, but it was playing by ear that gave him a looseness of spirit, even a joy as he trusted his ear, trusted his intuitions – hearing all the melodies, the chords, emerge without calculation as he hit the keys. "It's like walking downtown without knowing where I'm going. If it feels right to turn right I turn right, if it feels right to turn left I turn left, I trust myself, even when I play only on the black notes, it turns out OK."

❊   ❊   ❊

Al had dropped out of Harbord Collegiate to drive a truck for Donnie Ryan, an Irish cross-border bootlegger and cigarette smuggler.

Drinking Bushmill's whisky at the Hibernia Social Club in the Clinton Hotel and learning songs like "Who Put the Overalls in Mrs. Murphy's Chowder" he met a girl, Agnes Egan. She captivated him, telling him that her body was God's sacred vessel and then giving her body to him with no remorse at all, only pleasure, saying, "It's a sin between me and God, so I'll look after that." Because he made her pregnant, they married at City Hall and drove to Niagara Falls for their honeymoon, riding under the great falls on the *Maid of the Mist*, holding each other, soaking wet, seeing bits and pieces of rainbow light all around them in the mist, and Al decided he probably loved her, saying that he'd never seen such light. She clung to him and said she'd never seen such light either.

"Hail the light," he cried, happy.

"Shush," she said.

When Al returned to work, Donnie the bootlegger took him aside and told him he was fired, first for fucking a Catholic girl and then for marrying a Catholic girl.

"Regard me as old fashioned," the bootlegger said with an amiable wink of menace, "but you can't be nailing Our Lord Jesus Christ to the cross and then be nailing our women, too."

Al, at a loss for words, a loss that made him feel as if the things, the faces around him had gone numb, started to grin, and grinning he knew that he was going to do something, though he didn't know what he intended to do until he was in the midst of doing it.

Al broke Donnie's nose.

Then he threatened to kill a righteous young rebbe who told him God would curse his iniquity, He would punish such a marriage.

Al asked: "What kinda Jewish shit is that?"

The young rebbe said: "Ezekiel 18."

At the birth, Agnes and her boy child died, the child born strangled on his own cord, and Agnes dead from peritonitis.

Al said: "This is bullshit," and went to find the young rebbe and beat him with a sawed-off broomstick, cracking his ribs and collapsing his lung. "You got to believe God is crazy if you believe He strangles a child, you gotta be a lunatic to believe that," he told his father.

"There's a lotta lunatics," his father said.

"Count me out."

"In life, you gotta count for something somewhere," his father said.

"In life," Al said, "if I've got a thing with God, then it's me and God, it's not rules made up by somebody else. I've got what I get, I do what's to be done and I face up to it. That's it. That's all. Period. Punct."

To which his father said: *Gott bestraft die, die es verdient haben.* [1]

---

[1] God punishes those who deserve it.

And his mother said: *Es gibt niemanden, den Gott nicht bestraft.* [1]

"I don't believe any of this. I don't believe God punishes anyone."

❊   ❊   ❊

After Maxie Baker was attacked outside the Towne Tavern by Johnnie 'Pops' Papallia, who was working for the Maggadino family out of Buffalo, Al's father – who knew Baker because he bought newspapers from Marvin at the kiosk after doing his banking at the Imperial Bank on Temperance Street – introduced Al to Maxie.

Al said he liked Maxie's hat.

"It's a Harry Sable," he said, "one of my only indulgences. A man should wear a good hat."

"I'll get such a hat," Al said.

Maxie took off his hat and looked into it, as if there were something to be learned by looking into his hat. But he put it back on his head and laid his hand on Al's arm. "We'll take a little sun. Here we are, three Jews down among the bankers. I'll tell you something about the rich. The rich are rich because they play poor, they

---

[1] There is no one God doesn't punish.

give nothing away. They leave it to the poor to be generous, to give away what they ain't got."

"At big interest, too," Al's father said.

"The vigorish," Maxie said, "it's the national treasure. You know *The Treasure of Sierra Madre?*" he asked, "I love it. The world loves it. I love Humphrey Bogart when he says 'Conscience. What a thing. If you believe you've got a conscience it will pester you to death. But if you don't believe you've got one, what can it do to you?'"

"Bogart was a great actor," Al's father said, "great playing tough guys."

"Your father tells me you know how to be tough," Maxie said, putting his hand on Al's shoulder. "You don't brood. Brooding is the killer."

"If you happen to want to be a killer," Al said.

4

"You play a killer piano," the hunched old man said. "But I need to interrupt." He had laid his hand on Al's shoulder. At first, Al didn't move. Then, as he turned slowly on his stool he could tell the old man was a little drunk. He laughed. But there was also something cruel to the curl of the old man's lip. He looked, to Al, like a man who wanted to hurt someone, and if not someone, then he wanted to hurt himself. Al said, "This is supposed to be a happy time . . . ." but the old man had stepped on to the small dance floor and he said to the seniors in the room, "Today is August 2nd, sixty years to the day of the liberation of the camp at which I was an inmate – and several in this room were, too – the camp at Treblinka."

He straightened his body, drawing his heels together.

"Every day, ten times a day sometimes," the old man said, "when we were standing at attention on the Roll Call Square, thousands of us sang this song, that they'd drilled into us, singing till we were perfect, just like they wanted us to be, like a choir," and he began to sing in a droning monotone, in German, which Al understood:

> *This is why we are in Treblinka*
> *Whatever fate may send,*
> *This is why we are in Treblinka*
> *Always ready for the end.*

A man in the shadows at the back of the room called out, "Nobody needs this, sit down," and a woman yelled, "Shut up, sit down," but the old man kept on singing, unforgiving in his insistence, unforgiving of the other old people in the room, unforgiving of himself and, at the same time, insistent on his own humiliation.

"Stop," a man screeched. "For God's sake. You old fool."

> *Work is our existence*
> *We must obey or die.*
> *We do not want to leave . . .*

Someone threw a cane. The cane clattered against the piano as the old singer slumped into the stooped old man that he had been. Al said *Jesus Christ* to himself as he saw, sitting in an easy chair in the front row, Jake Piorko, looking weary but bemused, his jowls hanging loosely. Al spun on his stool and to break the awkward silence, he played and sang,

> *Embrace me, my sweet embraceable you,*
> *Embrace me, my irreplaceable you,*
> *Don't be a naughty baby,*
> *Come to papa, come to papa, do . . .*

❈   ❈   ❈

Al knocked, the door opened, and Al stepped into Jake Piorko's apartment. He took off his hat and brushed the nap of the pearl-grey crown with the forearm of his suitcoat. He said, "You need to know who I am."

"What are you talking? You I know, I hired you for God's sake."

"But even so, you need to know who I am."

With hands on hips, Jake leaned forward on his toes and looked into Al's eyes. "I know you," he said grimly. "You I seen a hundred times, it's in your eyes. So what's on your mind?"

"A bird. A parrot."

"That fucking bird. You're here because of that big-mouth bird? Dick Tracy would die laughing."

"Maybe you should be a little cautious."

"You're telling me, a ninety-year-old *alter kocker* who has outlived Hitler and a bunch of other shitheels who'd like my fucking head, that I should be cautious. You gotta be kidding."

"I don't kid."

"This, you'll pardon the expression, is strictly for the birds."

"There's a contract."

"So, you'll break my ninety-year-old arm. This is pathetic. You gonna kill me?"

"It seems."

"Likely story."

"That's what I want to know. What's the story?"

"I got no story. Nobody who comes out of the camps has got a story. We got details. I got seventy years of details. You're talking about I killed the bird. Sure, I killed the bird. This is an insult. You know how many thousands of men I seen killed."

"That's part of it."

"And so?"

"He says you were a *Kapo*."

"Big news. I'm supposed to worry, now, at this age, because back then, up to my nose in watery shit, I didn't swallow. That I'm alive. Fuck. I smell that shit every day of my life. Men. Women. I smell it on you, how do you like that? And he thinks that that bird of his is some kind of joke on somebody. It's no joke. And he thinks I should be sorry, for anything . . . ."

"Even so, we got a situation."

"Me, I'm all tired out. So you got a situation."

"That's right. A contract is a contract. I got to do what's got to be done. Otherwise it's an embarrassment."

"An embarrassment?"

"That's right."

"I can't believe this. I'm losing my mind."

"Maybe so."

"You're fucking *fermisshed*.[1] You want contract, I'll give you contract. All my money, what am I gonna do with it? Whatever he offered, I'll double it up. Turn it around, you want someone to kill, kill him! Put a parrot on his headstone."

Al put on his hat. "I can see I made a mistake," he said.

"The only mistake is if you don't take my price."

"I come to you," Al said, flushing with anger, "with a situation, trying to see if there could be some way to deal with this situation, and you make me a *shmear*, a cheap bribe that would make me a whore."

Jake sat down, crossed his legs, spread his arms, and looked around the room as if Al were not there, as if their confrontation was only a pause in a long weariness, and he turned back to Al and said, "Take off your hat, you're in my house."

Al was so taken aback by Jake's curtness that he took off his hat. Then he smiled indulgently at the quickness of his compliance, but before he could say anything Jake said, "I tell you the kinda detail you don't know nothing about. People talk about the camps, how all the deaths had no meaning, so God had to be dead, or maybe He never was. I got news for you, I said it then, I say it now,

---

[1] Confused

God was there. Auschwitz was as much His place as any other place, maybe more of His face was there than anywhere. I was no *tzaddic*, I refused to quit. I wasn't about to die, not in my own mind. I lived. I played the percentages. I stayed alive. The God of that place was with me, percentages that are a blessing, that's what a rebbe told me."

"Talking to God is crazy," Al said, uncertain of how to respond to the cold fury in Jake's eyes.

"So I tell you what I propose. Just like in the camp. I'll play you roulette."

He went to a side-table drawer and took out a gun. "Obviously I never lost . . . and so the deal is, I'll play and the stakes are this. If I win, I get whatever Harry put up for this job, plus the twenty that I had offered you which you now pay to me, but you don't have to do nothing.

"But if you lose . . . ?"

"I lose what I could've lost seventy years ago." He turned and opened the door to one of the empty rooms in the apartment. "In here," he said, "here I got everything going for me."

Al, following him and seeing only an entirely empty white room, said, "There's nothing here."

"You sure?"

"Nothing is nothing."

"Maybe God's here."

"There's no God."

"Say hello to *Hashem*,"[1] Jake said. "We got a deal?"

"I make you the contract."

Jake cracked open the gun, dropped six bullets into the palm of his hand, set one back into a chamber, and gave the cylinder a hard spin.

He put the barrel of the gun in his mouth and stood watching Al watch him. Jake took the barrel out of his mouth and with a contemptuous knowing smile said, "I think you're really gonna let me do it."

Al started to grin, he was playing the situation by ear, feeling sure of himself, that whatever was going to happen, it was going to happen as it should. Jake said, "Goddam, the way you're watching me, you're no different than the fucking SS," and he shoved the barrel in his mouth, pulled the trigger and blew out the back of his head.

❊ ❊ ❊

Harry and Al met in Switzer's Delicatessen. Harry was wearing a beautiful broad-brimmed black hat with a grey band, Al a caramel-brown felt fedora.

---

[1] The name

They ordered chicken soup and matzo ball, smoked meat sandwiches, a side of young dills, and cheesecake.

They said very little as they ate.

They ate, as did several orthodox men in the restaurant, while wearing their hats.

After coffee, Harry handed Al an envelope, ten thousand dollars in cash.

"Maybe this is how life ends," Harry said, "two *alter kockers* sitting together with lots to say about nothing. Mind you, if we were wops we'd have nothing to say about a lot."

Al handed the envelope back to Harry.

"There's no contract. What I did was nothing. It's got to be null. I was there, but I wasn't responsible."

"You sure about this?"

"Sure I'm sure. He loses, I lose, you win. As it should be."

"Except I got no Humbo, Humbo is dead, that fucking *Kapo*, he was no different than a Nazi . . . ."

"He told me I was a no different than the SS . . ."

"Out of his mind. Have a Remi Martin on me?"

"The drink of princes."

"Believe me, Al, you're a prince."

"Sure," Al said, "but wipe your lip, Harry, you got mustard on your lip, a guy with such a beautiful hat does not look good with mustard on his lip."

HEAD GAMES

When Gene Barlow was nine, the boy who lived across the street, Arnie Eacho, was fourteen. Arnie had a Daisy repeating air rifle that fired lead pellets. Gene said that to him the rifle looked like it could kill. Arnie said, "That's right, it can kill birds, even crows, and frogs and shoot out your eye." Gene said that he had never killed anything. Arnie said he would teach Gene how to kill. But first, Gene would have to let him suck his cock.

Gene made a noise like a frog, *ribbit ribbit*, which is the noise he made when he was asked a question he did not want to answer.

"We're playing for real here," Arnie said as he got down on his knees. Gene, dropping his jeans to his ankles, pretended to be a frog.

Taking hold of Gene's cock, Arnie said, "Think of Marilyn's tits."

Gene didn't know who Marilyn was. Her name sounded like a fish: *Marlin*. Instead, Gene thought of the long narrow red and yellow balloons his father always gave him after he had come home drunk and had slapped his mother, balloons his father twisted into the shape of men, the two red legs, the two yellow arms. Gene would pick up one of the balloon-men, light a match under his left leg or right arm – BOOM – and he'd sit laughing, holding the amputee in his hand.

"Look Dad, no feet."

Gene always laughed out loud at his joke because his father was a shoe salesman.

His father would cuff him on the back of the head and say, "Don't play me no head games. Where's your mother?" Gene knew his mother was hiding in the closet. His father, too, knew that she was in the closet. They left her alone. Gene was like his mother. He liked to be left alone. But then, when he thought about it, his father liked to be left alone, too. They all liked to be alone.

❁   ❁   ❁

His mother sometimes stood very erect, chin up, sing-ing, *Someone's in the kitchen with Dinah, someone's in the kitchen I know – ow –ow – ow.* Dinah was her name. But more often she crept quietly around the house. She had a tin box of Rolaid pastilles in her pocket, for heartburn. She took one and told him that she had come into his room and heard him in the night.

"Doing what?"

"Barking," she said.

"I barked?"

Gene had dreamed of a tightrope walker in a long dress standing on a white horse, the horse standing on a tightrope.

He had never been to a circus.

His mother asked him, "What did you dream last night?"

"About a horse and a tightrope."

"But before you woke up this morning you were barking like a dog."

"I don't know how to bark."

"And you said in your sleep, 'Barking keeps down the vermin.'"

She undid the top button of her blouse, the button at her throat, wanting air.

"So I bark?" he said.

"For real." she said.

She had begun to sing again:

Someone's in the kitchen . . .

He wanted to pray for her. The walls in the house were thin. Her panic passed from room to room like a whisper. Gene often thought he heard his mother asking him to pray for her through the walls. "Pray for me. I am afraid. God listens to children."

Nobody listens, he thought.

When his father wasn't drunk, his mother would say, "I'm trying to be happy," and his father would laugh and play little tunes on his mouth organ, a 10-dollar Hoener harmonica he could cradle tightly in one hand, and he held it up to his mouth as if his cupped hands were a nest, and inside, the bird never flushed from its nest unless his father gave up the bird, singing,

> *Say if I had wings*
> *Like a bullfrog on a pond*
> *I would fly away, fly*
> *Away in sweet mama's arms*

And then he would slip the harp into his pocket and Gene's mother would break into tears and go to bed and his father would call after her, "Try to be happy."

❉   ❉   ❉

It had been an August afternoon of dazzling white light. The white light filled Gene with a yearning for distant countries.

Arnie Eacho, looking up, said, "You're not trying."

Gene said, "Trying what?"

Arnie Eacho was angry. "I told you. Think of Marilyn's tits." Gene was afraid that Arnie was going to hurt him. He knew it was smart to be afraid of Arnie. Gene knew that there were a lot of boys like Arnie who were dangerous because – like his own father – they were angry all the time. He knew Arnie slashed tires, pissed on drunks sleeping in the street, had taken a sledgehammer to gravestones in cemeteries.

Gene's mother said, "But Arnie seems like such a nice boy," and Gene's father said, "Yeah, he's got get-up-and-go." Gene knew that there was a lot his mother and father didn't know.

But maybe, he thought, they knew who Marilyn was.

"Who's Marilyn?" he asked.

"Monroe, Marilyn Monroe . . . she killed herself," his mother said. "Why do you ask?"

"No reason."

He wondered why Arnie would have wanted him to think about a dead woman's tits.

Crazy, he thought.

❊   ❊   ❊

One week later, an old woman lost control of her car and drove into Arnie's house, going 80 or 90 miles an hour, and when Gene went to look at the smash-up, all he could see through the heavy steam coming out from under the hood was Arnie Eacho, who had sucked him off, and there was Arnie's head, sitting on top of the car's hood, eyes wide open, staring at Gene, and Gene, staring at Arnie, said, "Think about Marilyn," believing Arnie, no matter how angry, would get the joke, but when his father, who had come across the street, asked him, "What did you say?" he had nothing he wanted to say, so he said, "*Ribbit, ribbit,*" pretending he was a small boy.

A ONE-NIGHT STAND

From beyond the back porch light, he heard her laughter, and then he heard her coming up the porch stairs out of the rain, stepping in her slingback high heels along the narrow dimly lit hall of the small house he lived in, a house close to the lakefront rail lines, and she, holding her coat close, walked into the kitchen, heavy-breasted, a sauntering woman who had come back off the porch after breathing in for a few minutes the freshness of the early morning rain.

"It's still raining," Elise said.

"Who was you laughing with out there?" T-Bone asked.

"Myself," she said, "me and Philomena. We had a good laugh."

Her camel's hair coat fell open.

She had got out of bed naked and had put on her coat and gone outside onto the porch carrying Philomena, the rabbit puppet, under her arm. When she came back in, T-bone was seated at the kitchen table. He was in his shorts, wearing a shirt and a nylon stocking cap on his head, trying to keep the previous night's *conk* in his hair.

"I know I only know you since last night," she said, "but I still don't like you doing your head like that."

"I do what a black man do, girl, I gotta get my wig-hat on."

She opened a bottle of Jack Daniels that was on the table and poured herself a two-finger drink, neat.

"You drink like that" he said, "and you gonna get yourself a lifetime home in the ground."

He had a clouded whiteness in his left eye, but with his good eye he fixed on to her. She sat in silence, very still, along with the rabbit, Philomena, and let him stare at her until he broke the stillness by pouring himself a drink: "I'm gonna fry us up some T-bones, a T-bone and onions beats all for breakfast."

"You some kinda dude in the morning," Philomena said. She was suddenly sitting up straight on Elise's fist.

"In the morning's morning," T-bone said, leaning up close to the rabbit, "you is *one* mothafucka."

"No, no, I'm not the only one, for I come from a whole family of motherfuckers, Elise, she got the gift of tongues, she got hat boxes full of us."

❊   ❊   ❊

They had met at 2 in the morning on the outskirts of town. At that hour, after a gig, T-bone often went for a drive in his van "to slow down the bloods and arrive at some easement of mind." He'd stopped to fill up at the AC-DC Gas Bar & Groceteria where the fourteen trucking lanes of the 401 cross with the overnight commuter highway, 427. He was standing at pump Number 9 of the 11 cement Self-Serve islands, each island a pond of halogen light in the dark, and he was staring at island 8 where a white woman – as she pumped gas into her red Passat – wore on her left hand, hanging head-first down, a puppet glove, a floppy-eared rabbit, and he saw the rabbit's mouth flap and heard a voice by his right shoulder ask, "What's happening?" so he called across the cement island, "Be cool," and when the woman, still holding the gas nozzle to her tank turned to look at him, he said, "You one of them ventriloquists, like on TV?"

"Maybe."

"You wanta do some personal damage?"

He racked his nozzle.

"He's probably one of those nighttime crazies," the rabbit called out.

"Not me," T-bone said, coming across the island.

"I foresaw who you were, coming at me," she said.

"You saw me?"

"Right."

"What's my name then?"

"T-bone Duflet."

"How'd you know that?"

"It's all over your wheels, man."

He turned to face *T-bone Duflet & His Blues Band* on the side of his van.

"There I be," he said, laughing.

"You a good man or a bad man?"

"I be what I do," he said, "I sing the song."

❀   ❀   ❀

He shifted his iron-ware pan on the gas fire as he kept on telling her about his home farm and his father, and how he had watched his father die slowly, the dying so slow it was like studying rain. "There's all kinds of rain," he said. "There's rain in your heart, and there's rain that comes out of the woods in sheets and in the springtime it looks like ghosts, long tall ghosts, and that's what white people were like, too," he said, "ghosts," and he winked at her, "long and tall," and then he started telling her about his Uncle Lazarus. "I was a Lazarus by name, too, until I became T-bone at the piano, but meanwhile," he said, "my uncle was a man who had himself an alligator mouth and because of his mouth he had got his own self in trouble with a good-looking white woman. She was a lot like you," he said, "except where we are now ain't the way it was back then because back then the sheriff had lit out after Lazarus, his dogs whooping, and when they finally did corner old Lazarus' hummingbird ass, the sheriff he hollers, 'You're a dead man, Lazarus,' and Lazarus come up into the open from between two trees and calls, 'I been betwixt and between before,' and the sheriff shoots him but he comes back one more once between two other trees like he's never been shot. 'You're a dead man, Lazarus,' and the sheriff shoots him but Lazarus keeps coming up while they say he's running farther away, coming back, and running away in the rain till they never did find him or find his ghost," and T-bone, pleased with himself, pleased with the look of admiration in her eyes for his storytelling, said, "And Lazarus, he keep coming on every springtime, he one of those long tall ghosts of rain," and then he whispered a song to her,

> . . . *consumption killing me by degrees*
> *I can study rain*

❆   ❆   ❆

In the turned down lamplight of his bedroom they had undressed, unhurried, at 3 in the morning. The bed had newel posts. She had looked around for a place to rest the rabbit, Philomena, and then had sat her with her hanging ears straight up, alert, over one of the posts. In that shadow light on the bed she had drawn her knees back to her shoulders, trying to take him in deeper, and he'd cried, "You mine, baby, you is all mine," but she had thought, the pain of his deepness giving her pleasure, *No, this is mine,* and she had rolled him over, surprising him with her unexpected strength, and then she'd sat on top of him and said, "Mine," at last, in release, falling forward over him, kissing his neck, saying, "Turn up the light, baby. I wanta see you, I've never been with a black man before."

"You is with a lady killer," he said, laughing.

"Don't you worry yourself," he heard Philomena say from the post, "she's so quick you won't know she was here til she's gone."

As he reached for the light, she eased back off his body, sliding down between his feet, to sit beside Philomena.

"Here I am down at the deep end," she said, surprised to see that the whole length of one wall beside the bed was a mirror.

In a fuller light, with his eyes accustomed to the light, he said, "Jesus, Lord," leaning forward to look at her more closely.

Below the glitter of a rhinestone in her navel, he saw that she had shaved all her body hair, she was bald at the cunt except for a razor-thin line of black hair. "It's called the California cut," she said.

He drew his finger along the line of hair. "Ain't life a bitch," he said and he rolled her over on to her stomach, buckled her knees, and entered her, saying, "Gonna get me some more trim," not with the lunge of the earlier hour, but slowly, and then he heard from behind her shoulder, the rabbit, "You sure she wants to do this this way?"

"Lord Jesus," he said, and collapsed on her back, and she burst out laughing and he laughed, too, and he said, "Next time, the rabbit stays in the next room."

She took him into her arms. "Sorry about that," she said, "it's just my way of talking, can't help it, it's me."

With her cheek against his neck she felt something like a moaning inside his throat and when she asked what was the matter, he said, "Never you mind, girl, it be raining . . . ." She didn't know what to say, so she said, "Not telling's unfair." So he hauled back out of her arms, at being told he was unfair, but laughing as if by laughing he was putting something protective between them, a protection being necessary be-cause they didn't know each other at all, and then he said with a weariness of tone that left her speechless, "Ain't noth-ing more foolish-looking than a black man with his head on a white woman's shoulder."

They kept their silence for a long time. Then he touched his fingers to her lips.

"We's alright, we here, baby," he said. "An' I gonna make you mine."

"You don't have the time," she said.

"All the time ain't no time at all."

"You know what I notice," she said, "you got, like, no pictures, nothing at all on the walls or anywhere in your room, you got a lot of nowhere behind you."

"I got nowhere everywhere and I want all of it be-hind me. I put a lotta bad shit behind me. There some-where you got to be?"

She was sitting on the edge of the bed, facing the mirror, at ease, her legs bent open, the rhinestone in her navel a point of light in the mirror.

"I don't need to take nothing from you, T-bone," she said, "and I got nothing to give that's more than what I already gave."

"Fair 'nough," he said. "I ain't asking."

"Fair's got nothing to do with it."

"Maybe you gotta check it out with the rabbit!"

She laughed and took both his hands in hers and put them to her lips.

"What you do with your hands, the way you play, is beautiful."

"How you know?"

"I've heard you play, I didn't just say hello at the gas bar for no reason."

"Your rabbit said hello."

"Tomorrow it would have been Wilbur. Like Philomena said, I got a whole box of boys and girls."

"You crazy, girl. How I gonna talk to you when I don't know who is gonna answer me?"

"Hell, I don't know how to talk to myself," she said.

Side-by-side, facing the mirror, she said, "I hate mirrors, my mother, she used to look in the mirror after she'd had a drink and she'd say like she was real angry that she was looking for the child she'd lost, my twin sister, who'd died beside me stillborn, and sometimes she'd see my sister in the mirror and talk to her all night like we're talking now, trying to get her to come out from behind the glass and if my mother was drunk enough she'd call her out by her name, Lisa, and call her a coward for hiding behind the mirror and then she'd put her arms around me and hold me and call on Lisa to quit carrying on like some kind of ghost but when mother got so altogether wound up and confused in the circles of her own mind she'd hold me and call me Lisa instead of Elise, like she was holding a dead girl who had come back to life in her arms."

"Hey, I wasn't holding no dead girl," T-bone said, and he then brushed her blonde hair away from her eyes and laid her back on the bed, "No dead girl was rattling my bones," and cradling her in his arms, he entered the cradle of darkness again hearing her say, "Oh."

❃   ❃   ❃

With the morning rain coming down in sheets, constant, a chill had come on, taking hold in the kitchen.

T-bone, after turning on the stove's gas burners, and putting bread in the toaster, two steaks and onions in the big pan, had dressed for warmth in his tuxedo suit-coat, the same coat he wore every night while playing at the Show Bar, a coat that was one size too big for him, the sleeves hanging down to his knuckles. He'd worn the old coat for years and he told her he thought it had once belonged to an undertaker because of the broad, black silk band sewn around the left sleeve. "Unless maybe it was a suit for a one-armed bandit and when he died that's how they sewed the sleeve back together."

"So you're my dead man walking," she said.

"Now you hip to what it's like to sleep with the dead."

He did a little shuffle dance of delight at his own wit in front of the stove.

"We're some pair in the morning," she said, "I drink and you dance."

"We's the best, girl. Cool as the breeze on Lake Louise."

"I caught the heel of my shoe out there on the porch," she said. "Thought I snapped it off. They say if you break the heel off your shoe in the morning you're gonna meet the love of your life by nightfall. But I didn't break my heel."

"You gonna break my heart, woman, talking at me like that."

"I just bet you're in love with me."

"Dunno 'bout love, but I *am* a lover."

"Yes you are, and it seems like a miracle to me."

"What kinda miracle?"

"I wasn't looking for no special thing last night, I was looking to gas up and go home. A night as common as dirt could be."

"Uh-huh."

He shook lemon pepper onto the two T-bones and onions, set them down on a platter between two plates and poured two glasses of bourbon, but instead of sitting down, he started to poke about the kitchen as if he was looking for something that he had forgotten, his shoulders slumped inside his coat.

She let him turn in a circle and turn in a circle again and then she said, "What you looking for, what you lose?"

He said, "I'm looking for something I lost in my mind, Captain Hook, I'm looking for when I was a kid in love with myself and I believed back then that I was a tall mothafucker who had killed Captain Hook with one blow of my fist to his eye-patch and when I looked under his eye-patch this small snake was nested right there in his eye socket and that snake bit me on my cheek and I have a small scar," and T-bone touched his cheek, "right here that I tell people is a birthmark but I'm telling you that it is the mark of the snake's tongue."

She reached out and took hold of him by the sleeve that had the black silk arm band. "The night before yesterday," she said, "I dreamed I was sound asleep but my bed was gone. I was asleep in mid-air."

"What's that supposed to mean?" he asked, sitting down.

"I don't know. You study your rain, I just deal with what has to be dealt with, the way things are, or the way things are sometimes waiting to be something else – a spiral, a girl on a bench who thinks she is a violin. What has to be dealt with is miracle enough."

He hit the table with the heel of the knife handle he held in his fist, making her flinch and draw back.

"Try staying alive."

"What?"

"That's what I deal with. And talking to myself. All that other shit's too much for me."

"Talking to yourself is what lonesome people do."

"When Philomena is talking," he asked, an acid edge to his tone as he cut into his T-bone, "is she talking to you or is that you talking to yourself."

"Sometimes she talks," she said, "and I don't know what she's saying til she says it."

"Maybe, girl, you want to try travelling light."

"What's that?"

"Take it from me, too many people taking turns talking inside your head tires you down. Takes your breath away."

"God," she said, "listen to him."

"Sounds like a sentence of life to me," Philomena said, lifting her head from Elise's lap.

"Sometimes," T-bone said, "I close my eyes and I see something like maybe the way it was with us last night. And then I open my eyes and you and me, we aren't nowhere to be found, like the man say when I was a kid out on the street, 'Make yourself scarce, boy,' and what I've found out as I've come up in life is that being scarce is being free."

"You playing scarce with me?"

"Naw, girl, you is fine. You my woman this day."

"I ain't nobody's woman," she said, "not yours, not my momma's, not my sister's, not nobody's."

"You watch out, girl, you ain't gonna die from nothing like consumption, you got rain in your heart that's gonna kill you."

She said nothing, feeling a terrible heaviness in her chest, a swelling weight that she'd often felt before, but it wasn't any kind of illness, it wasn't rain, it probably was, she thought, the hand of her dead mother on her heart, a heavy coldness that would creep up into her throat, a weight so cold that she wished she could get out of her body and stay out until the coldness went away. But she never wanted to ever finally leave her body. She liked her body, she liked to think about her sauntering walk, it gave her a warmth, a feeling of allure when she was naked. She liked the sound of the word, allure, especially seeing how eager, how in want, T-bone had been when she had taken off her clothes. She'd stood and let him look, taking her own pleasure at him looking. Then, sitting there in the kitchen, she remembered that under the coat she had no clothes on. She slid her hand inside her coat and touched her breast thinking she and T-bone should be naked together again in bed, but she was afraid that if she went to the bedroom again to make love she would find Lisa sitting in the mirror waiting for her. She'd left her skirt, her sweater, her panties on the floor at the base of the mirror. She decided she was going to leave them there, she wasn't going to take a chance on finding Lisa waiting for her.

"My time ain't most people's time," T-bone said, "the nighttime be the right time for me. The rest of the time is day, and they's different people that live in a different city in the day. The same city but a different city. Some peoples feel 'fraid at night, Lord Jesus," he said clapping his hands, staring at her out of his clouded eye, a little confused as she sat wrapped in her camel's hair coat, blonde hair combed straight to her shoulders, the rabbit puppet in her lap, and he said, "Even so . . . ."

"Even so what?"

"I woke up thinking about my daddy."

"You think your daddy would like me?"

"The point is, can you remember my daddy?

"How could I?"

"'Course you can't."

"You mean 'cause I'm white."

"I mean I'm all my daddy's got. His whole life was the nighttime. My ghosts don't talk to your ghosts, you got daytime ghosts."

"I got Philomena," she said.

"And she be only a ghost of herself," he said, and he began to laugh, and laugh loud, so he could hardly talk for laughing. And she started to laugh. She couldn't figure out what he was laughing at but she laughed along with him.

He said, "You is fine, girl, fine."

"I don't know what you are," she said.

"Maybe after our T-bones we should go back to bed and do the real T-bone."

"No time," the rabbit rising up from her lap said.

"Shut your mouth," she said, and smacked Philomena in her head. She fell forward into Elise's lap again, whining, saying, "It's morning, you got to go, you got a performance this afternoon."

"A performance?" T-bone asked.

"Yes," she said. "I do kids' shows, too. Birthdays in the garden, that kind of stuff. I love it. The kids love it. They talk to Quack Quack the Duck and Mister Magoo . . . whatever glove I've got on, whatever face, it's hilarious, those kids want to know some mean things, about life . . . what's going on . . . ."

"An' you tell them . . . ."

"I explain the whole world. Or at least, Quack Quack the Duck does . . . ."

"And Philomena listens . . . ."

"Philomena never listens, she sits behind me and smiles."

"I got too much of everything behind me," T-bone said, and then he reached across to Elise and took her hand, lifting it to his lips, and said, "What I do is sing the song, girl," and he tasted the soft flesh between her fingers, tonguing the little web of flesh, holding her eye with his, and then he said, almost growling at her, "You don't know . . . you can't know nothing about me, nothing about what I be doing when I play, when I sing the song, 'cause when I sing about all the ghosts I got in me, I am Lazarus . . . I am the fucking resurrection of the dead."

He picked up his knife and fork to finish eating his steak. She had not touched her meat. She had the feeling she could smell the dead. The dead with onions. She took a lipstick from her pocket and while T-bone cut up his meat she half-turned away from him and slowly reddened her mouth. She licked her lips, she liked the taste of herself. She said she thought she might go out and take a little air again on the porch with Philomena, she wanted to be there in case anybody came back from the dead before it stopped raining.

She picked up her car keys.

"That's a good looking T-bone you leaving there," he said.

She said that maybe she would come back but not to eat. She walked down the dark hallway. T-bone, who was working hard with his knife around the bone of his steak, could hear the click click of her high heels. "Sweet meat's close to the bone," he called out, wagging his knife at the door to the hallway. "I got to get me a light in that hall, man." He picked up the bone and chewed it. "She sure do have her own hummingbird bootie," he said aloud, and set down the bone.

DÉJÀ VU

I wonder what I'll do now that I have seen the room where I was born in several black-and-white B-movies where there is a hotel room in the east end of town down by the old railroad station and there is a single bed, an iron cot against the wall, and on the floor, an old leather suitcase that has been made up into a child's bed, my bed, and outside, there's a hotel sign that flashes on and off, which, after my mother, a brunette with high cheekbones, has gone downstairs to the bar, turns out later in the movie to be the Hotel Rex. The bartender, a retired light-heavyweight boxer who has a moon face and a bent nose, has always favoured my mother for what he says is her beautiful skin. She smiles at him. "Peaches and cream," she says, touching his hand, and then touching her cheek, "peaches and cream. That's how life should be." She smokes a Camel, tapping her ash into a heavy glass ashtray, and she blows a smoke ring and turns on her barstool, crossing her legs, and she says, looking me dead in the eye, "Don't you worry, boy, when the world ends, the world's gonna end on B-flat."

THE HARDER
THEY COME

Crede Doucet had his mother's very pale blue eyes, but he was long in the jaw and lean and bony and gaunt. She was plump. His father, Eldon Doucet, a well-known lawyer, who also was long in the jaw, and lean, said, "How come he never has a good word for me?"

"He envies you," his wife, Madeleine, said, "the way you're so satisfied with your own life."

"A man gets what he deserves," he said, unbuttoning his blue serge vest, as he always did at the end of the afternoon, sitting down in his wingback chair.

"Sometimes, Eldon," she said, "you sound more like a judge than a lawyer."

"Life," he said, running his hand through thinning hair, "is like politics. Once you start explaining, you're finished, and I've been trying to explain myself to that boy for years."

"We don't agree. And he's not a boy. He's twenty-seven."

Because she turned away, Eldon thought he had upset her but she had only turned to admire the sitting-room's new pinstripe wallpaper, a paper she had picked out at Ye Olde Shoppe to mark their 30th wedding anniversary.

It has a quiet dignity, she thought. And even better, a necessary dignity.

※　　※　　※

"I never really knew my father either," Eldon said. "He was a man who liked ballroom dancing and ties. That much I knew. He had hundreds of ties. Before he died – perhaps it was some kind of joke – he gave every last one of his ties to a charity drive for the homeless."

She poured him a cup of strong green tea. No milk. No sugar.

He believed green tea was good for his bowels. He worried about his bowels.

He watched for a yellowing under his eyes.

He watched for blood in his stool. Liver spots on his skin. He said he wasn't worried about being dead, it was whether dying would humiliate him, how he was going to die.

"I rather liked my father," she said, sipping a well-watered scotch. As usual, she had been slow-sipping all afternoon. "He was a nice man, nice to every woman he met except my mother. Then I grew up and got over her disappointment. I discovered I had my own disappointments."

"Growing up isn't enough."

"It helps."

"Crede's a grown man and you still encourage him, still think he's going to be some kind of singer, keeping all those old scrapbook pictures of him in his opera outfits, Othello, for God's sake. A tenor in black face. Othello was no tenor. It was a joke."

"He has a wonderful voice," she said. "I love his voice."

He sat back and sipped his tea, expecting her to say something cutting, but she surprised him. She slipped off her shoes and touched his thigh, saying, "I wonder what he'll be like when we're dead?"

"It's all in the family, in the blood," he said. "Seeing as we called him Crede, just like my father. My father was a hard man. I didn't know how different Crede'd be. He breaks my heart. It's like he's turned his back on who he is, hanging out at the race track. Nobody goes to the race track every day, only touts and layabouts."

"And the owners," she said wryly.

"He should own up to how he's ruining his life."

"Maybe so," she said. "Maybe so."

He said nothing.

There were times when saying nothing was best. He worried that he might have sounded petulant.

"Maybe he'll be more like us than we'd like to know," she said.

"He has to take hold of himself," he said firmly.

"Anyway, come to bed."

*   *   *

In bed, he was puzzled by the quiet care she took to make love to him, as if she were gently amused, so that he was self-conscious and made no sound, afraid to sigh, watching and waiting as if something quite separate from their lives was going to happen, and he was so upset and softened by her agreeable smile as he drifted off to sleep that he wondered how he might get close to her again . . . he believed they had been wonderfully close . . . . But the next morning as she left for her swim at the Rosedale Ladies Club, she said, "Don't you think it's nice the way we can accommodate each other without too much emotion."

That night he made love to her with a cold fury that frightened him, it was like the fury he felt at times in the courtroom as he closed in on some despicable lying cheat slouched on the stand, a fury that one day had caused him to say out loud, triumphantly, before the bench, "This is how we keep the low-life down," eliciting a reprimand from the judge; but then he eased off her body in their bed and he went to sleep staring straight up at the ceiling, feeling helpless after she said, "That was nice," and kissed him lightly on the cheek. "Sleep tight," she said.

❊   ❊   ❊

It was a Saturday afternoon. She and Crede were at the front of the garden. Under an apple tree. She planted the tree after he'd been born. It was her favourite corner of the garden, protected from the wind by the tree. His father stood alone at the back of the garden by the peony beds. He was looking to see if the blooms were heavy with black ants. Black ants brought peonies fully to bloom. Sitting at a wrought-iron table that had a glass top, his mother was playing double solitaire.

"When did you start wearing your bathrobe out to the garden?" she asked Crede.

"I dunno."

"Naked underneath!"

"How'd you know?"

"A mother knows when her boy is naked."

"Red eight on the black nine," Crede said.

"I almost never beat this game," she said.

"Why play? Nobody beats double solitaire."

"That's not the point. The point is you keep playing or else you just quit, you wake up in the morning, 'So long solitaire.' Like someone says *so long* in the night. You wake up and say, 'So long, too . . . .' And no one answers. You're on your own."

"I'm here."

"And your father's here."

"King on the ace. Of clubs."

Crede lowered his head and said quietly, "Long live the King."

Then he laughed and she shushed him and said, "We are being quite naughty about the man I love."

"I know, I know."

"The thing is, your father, when he wakes in the morning, he's always afraid that something will have gone missing in the night, afraid everything won't be exactly where he left it. Myself, I'm disappointed that a whole night has gone by and nothing has got lost, that everything's where it was."

"And still is," he laughed.

She raised her empty glass.

"Red queen on a black king," he said, and reached under the table for the whisky thermos and poured her a drink.

"A well-watered scotch," she said, as if explaining. "Thank you."

"Think nothing of it."

"In the old days, this," she said, holding the glass high with an air of triumph, "would have been laudanum. All the respectable ladies of the time got blissful indeed on laudanum. Opium got a lady through the day."

"Sometimes I think you're happy being unhappy."

"Who said I'm unhappy? It's just that when I'm cold sober I hear the *tock tock* of the clock. Too loud, too clear. *Tock. Tock. Tock.* Drive you crazy. *Tock. Tock. Tock. Tock. Tock* . . . ."

"Cut it out."

"Why? *Tock. Tock.*"

"It's irritating."

"It's the sound your father's heart makes at night."

"Now you are drunk."

"I am not. Your father listens to his liver and his heart but he keeps his eye on you, he told me he thinks you want to kill him."

"He's who he is and I don't want to kill him, I just don't want to be him. That's all. He thinks he's gone missing in my life if I don't end up like him."

"Maybe in the morning, I'll be among the missing persons."

"That sounds goddam unhappy to me."

"No, no. You've got it all wrong. My idea of hell is being locked up for life in a room with a happy man. A world of sunlight, with no moon. Who could stand it?"

"God?"

"Nonsense. God sneaks around in the dark in secret."

His father, flipping open the gold lid to his pocket timepiece, called out, "Two o'clock. Watch the heat. The double peony blooms are spectacular, full of ants."

"Oh good," she said and stood up and began to waltz alone on the grass, holding the hem of her dress with one hand, circling Crede, singing, holding her whisky glass with the other,

My heart cries for you,
sighs for you,
please come back to me . . .

stopping, pointing at his father with the hand that held the glass, "And don't forget he's a detail man, and such," she said, taking hold of Crede in her arms, "such are the details of my disappointment."

She laughed, as if her laughter were an admission that she had found satisfaction in an acceptance of who she had become while her husband, not knowing what she had said, came toward them, handling the weight of his pocket watch before slipping it into his vest-pocket.

"Everything in his life, even time," she whispered, "he plays close to the vest."

※   ※   ※

Two weeks later, she was found in her bathing suit with her neck broken, dead, sprawled on the sky-blue tiles of the Rosedale Ladies Club swimming pool. The caretaker had drained the pool for repairs and had forgotten to lock the door into the room that glared with summer light from the wide glass roof.

"Sometimes," the caretaker said, "even when it's filled with water you feel you're diving into the sky. She mustn't have looked down."

His father, to clear aside any confusion over how or why she died, called for an inquiry.

The coroner said, "She took a dive," and ruled Accidental Death.

For two afternoons, Crede sat in the garden under the apple tree: he had a feeling that just behind him, if he were to whirl around, he would find an open seam in the air, open to a silent scream he knew was there, a scream he was trying to hear; but he did not hear it, he waited, and torn between fury and lethargy, aching with loss, he sat hunched through two afternoons of drizzle, hollow-eyed, bedraggled, bleak, as close as he had ever come to what he thought was prayer. On the second day his father stood for a while beside him in the light rain, but then said, "For Christ's sake, man," and went back into the house.

On the morning of the funeral, Crede showered, shaved with a straight razor, scrubbed his hands, and trimmed his nails until his forefinger bled. Sitting on the toilet, he licked the blood from his finger. He liked the taste of his blood. He had always licked the blood whenever he'd cut himself as a child. His mother had told him his saliva helped to heal the wound. He liked the idea of healing himself.

At the requiem Mass in the cathedral under the tall yellow brick steeple he looked flushed, eager and enormously pleased as he tilted his head to look back over the crowded pews. "You look like you're counting the house," his father said sternly, admonishing him, but then added, as if happily content with a public respect being shown to his family, "it's really quite a crowd."

During the requiem Mass, Crede stared straight ahead, moving his lips, but not, his father realized, to the lilt of the prayers. "Are you talking to yourself?" his father asked, gripping the pew. Crede smiled and patted his hand. "No, not to myself." Then, he startled his father by leaving the pew and getting into the line going to communion. His father knew that no one in the family had gone to confession for years, and though he was not ardent in his faith, he nonetheless believed in rituals – after all, he said, the Law was made up of those rituals that had been codified through centuries of inquiry, just as the Church through its Councils and Encyclicals had codified itself, always looking back to and consulting its great Fathers, Aquinas and Augustine, as the Law looked back to and consulted its great Fathers, Gladstone and Holmes.

"You're in a state of sin," his father whispered, and then he went rigid with indignation as he realized that Crede had stepped out and away from the pew again and he was going back up to the altar, to stand on the carpeted altar, something he'd obviously arranged with the Monsignor; but there'd been no consultation with him, no consideration of what he might have wanted; he had been left out and he tasted a sourness, a bile come up in his throat; "Goddam my bowels," he said as Crede concluded the celebration of the Mass by singing the *Panis Angelicus:*

> *Panis angelicus*
> *Fit panis hominum;*
> *Dat panis coelicus*
> *Figuris terminum;*

O res mirabilis!
Manducat dominum

❊   ❊   ❊

Eight months after his mother's death, stepping out of the steaming shower stall in the morning, shivering with the shock of cold air, Crede put on his heavy white terry-cloth robe with a shawl collar, and his soft black leather slippers, brushed his closely cropped hair and then paused at the head of the stairs below the stained-glass window, the strong morning light dappling his skin with rose and emerald petals. He listened to his father shuffling barefooted behind his closed bedroom door, getting on and off the scale that he kept beside his bed.

"First thing in the morning and he's checking the weight of the world," he said to himself, laughing quietly, and then he yelled, "I think you're getting slower and slower each morning," as he went down the carpeted stairs to cook breakfast, which he now did every morning, cracking four eggs into a bowl and reaching for any one of the copper pans which hung from the steel hooks over the stove.

They ate across from each other at an old pine table, with a single pink rose between them in a pressed-glass vase that his mother had bought. The breakfast room had a sliding glass door to the garden and the door was full of morning sunshine, and the soft light fell on his father's flushed pink face.

"Well," said Crede wryly, "here we go again, alone together."

"Yes. So we've been."

He looked down at his plate.

"Yes, I must say," he said, touching the yellowing pouches under his eyes, "I am not ready to be alone."

They sat in silence, neither eating.

Then: "You cook a good egg, Crede," he said. "Your mother always cooked a good egg."

"You make it sound like she was a good egg."

"She was herself a damn good woman," he said, smoothing rosehip jelly onto his toast. "In her own way, she could deal with things. She could deal with me and she certainly dealt with you." He bit into the toast and chewed slowly. "I'd call leaving you all her money a damn good nest egg."

"I wonder what bothers you most," Crede said. "Whether it was Mother leaving me the money, or not telling you she was going to give me the money."

"What bothers me," he said, slipping his knife into the heart of the jelly jar, "is that you not only refuse to work but you don't have to work."

"I sing," he said, lifting the pink rose out of the vase, putting it to his nose and inhaling deeply with his eyes closed.

"Sing, my ass. You haven't taken a lesson or sung on stage for over a year. Playing the gentleman punter at the track . . . ."

"I sing every day," he said. "I sing you home from work and you don't even like it. Here," and he snapped the long green stem and handed the rose to his father. "Put this in your lapel."

"A rose by any other name," his father said softly, with great control, and then, buttoning his vest for the trip downtown to his office, he said: "Don't forget, tomorrow is Wednesday. Wednesday night."

Crede got up: "I won't forget, Father."

Putting the rose in his lapel his father said, "Do you know I spent yesterday afternoon with Senator Mulroney in my office. Life's little fixer, they call him, and he was courting me. You know what that means? That smooth man, he believes in nothing except his own smoothness, but when I looked at myself in the mirror this morning I saw what I believe in."

"And what's that?"

"Me, and I liked what I saw, and I see a lot of me in my neighbours but I don't see you in me."

✽   ✽   ✽

His father had quick darting eyes and a small cleft in his long chin that gave him an air of severity, which he himself saw as dignified and women seemed to find attractive.

He always wore a dark double-breasted suit with a grey silk tie, and carried his gold pocket watch in his vest. He believed the only slight he'd ever suffered, a slight in the sense that someone had actually hurt him and laughed in his face, was the day after Crede had been born, when he'd felt something so close to a seizure of light-headed gaiety, a feeling of affirmation, that – in a moment of spontaneous playfulness – he'd worn a pair of his own father's spats to the office. His partner had laughed, telling him: "If only you were a nigger you'd look like a pimp."

He'd never forgiven his partner his hoot of loud laughter, and unbuttoning the spats that night he'd decided – thinking what a fine judicious man his father had been – to call his son by the name of Crede – to make sure that what he stood for and what his father had stood for (if nothing else, a stern sense of decorum) would continue. But now they were both dead, his wife and the partner – a pair of spats in the ground, he'd suddenly thought at the requiem Mass, a little

afraid of his own levity as he'd grimly held on to the
pew, touched by an unfamiliar sense of pity for all their
lives – as if for a moment he believed that their lives
were only caprice, a coming and going, a buttoning and
unbuttoning, and despite the indignation he'd felt
standing alone in the pew, he had been moved almost to
tears by his son's singing at the end of the Mass, admir-
ing his determination, his loyalty to his mother, even
while regretting the thinness of Crede's voice, as if that
thinness – a tenor verging on falsetto – was a reflection,
a thinness that told everyone – and the telling filled him
with a panic, with the need to be with another woman
– that he had been incapable of any intemperate fullness
of expression in his own life.

❧   ❧   ❧

At six o'clock on that afternoon, Tuesday, Crede – who
had been to the race track and had come home and had
showered – stood beside his bedroom window in his
terry-cloth dressing gown. He lifted the lid on a CD
discography cabinet and selected Pavarotti and – as he
often did during the week, as a part of his little ritual
with his father – he turned on the sound system, the
compact powerful speakers mounted on either side of
him at the window.

Through the leaves of the maple tree he could see his father step spryly on to the flagstone front walk, coming home. Crede pulled the silver sound lever forward and sang along with Pavarotti, singing as loud as he could, throwing his arms wide open, and the street swelled with the song of blended voices, a splendour that his father took as it was intended, as a taunt, as Crede stood staring through the maple leaves remembering how his mother had held his boy-child hand by that same window while they watched a cat prowl through the branches and she'd said, "Cats never show that they're grateful for the love they've been given, not unless it's when they leave a dead bird at the door, like a gift." She had shrugged and laughed. "Men never understand that love can be the sharing of something dead."

His father turned sharply from the walk and into the garage and came out a few minutes later. And though it was chilly with the tang of late fall on the wind, he was in his shirt-sleeves, dragging the gas lawn mower out to the garden, to the lawn he kept closely cropped until the first snow. "You can lawn bowl on a green like this," his beaming father often said to his neighbours, though he'd never bowled in his life, and with a wry, cold smile he yanked the cord and turned on the clacking-clattering power mower.

The sound sheared through the air, and he stood for a moment looking up into the leaves that shielded Crede's window from the street, and Crede stepped back into the shadow of his curtains, watching as his father slowly guided the mower back and forth, drowning out the music until Crede closed the window and sat down in a crouch, his robe falling open and, legs apart, he saw himself naked in the long mirror on the closet door. He was startled, as if seeing himself for the first time, startled by how dark his crotch hair was, black against his pale skin, and how lost in the darkness was his cock. He said quietly, wistfully, "Mother."

✳   ✳   ✳

Within eight months of Crede planting flowers on his mother's grave, within eight months of the silences he and his father had shared, feeling each other's awkwardness, his father had said, "Enough is enough," and he had brought his new lady home for high tea, fixing Crede with a look of stern satisfaction as she'd said, "My name is Grace."

She had thick black hair and a supple shapeliness, and though she was dressed in a tailored dark suit and wore black leather gloves – gloves that were out of fashion but gave her an air of professionalism – there was a sly impishness in the way she sat on the arm of an easy chair and, while smoking a gold-tipped Nat Sherman cigarette, said, "I never inhale, I just like the gold tips."

She sat smoothing her dress on her thigh, artfully detached and drawn into herself, aware that in her silence both men were watching her. "You're staring," his father said, and Crede said, "Yes, I suppose I am. Sorry."

She rose and offered Crede her gloved hand and then, kissing him lightly on the cheek, said, "There's no need to be sorry, only men who don't know what they have done should say they're sorry." Her hair caught all the light from the sitting-room bay window. Then she said: "The wallpaper in this room looks just like a bank manager's suit." She smiled, amused by her own audacity, and his father seemed to be amused, too.

"That wallpaper was thirty years in the making," Crede said, "but never mind."

Because it was Wednesday evening – his father's time to be alone in the house with Grace – as dusk came on, Crede had taken a glass of white wine with pâté and Cumberland sauce and then he had driven east, past the soybean mills and cross-country courier depots, and a spray-painted scrawl on a precast concrete wall: GOD IS DEAD AND HE DOESN'T CARE, out to Ashbridges Bay, to the old gabled racetrack on the lakeshore. He had a reserved chair in one of the clubhouse boxes. He sat with his arms folded as he watched the line of horses and their leads come up out of the dark tunnel from the paddock on to the track.

He loved, in the closing light of dusk and the light from the overhead flood lamps, the sheen of sweat on the chest muscles and forelegs of the horses, and he was certain he could tell, as he peered through his big army war-surplus binoculars, whether a horse was ready to run well or whether it was washed out, dripping sweat. He liked to see a prick to the ears of a horse and never bet on fillies.

Sometimes, he left his box and went on to the club-house floor to feel the mood among the players, and wearing one of his elegantly cut double-breasted Milan linen jackets, he stood listening among men that he had casually come to nod hello to over recent years, familiar faces with no names, and he liked the brief intimacy of their shared intensity that required no names, that required only a willingness to listen and then to play and then forget among fast-talkers with their pocket computers who fed each other fractions and formulas, their fingertips smudged with ink from the Racing Form, all locked into their own systems of speed ratings and past performances, as if somehow – in trying to win – there were ways to locate a length lost in a past race that would, if found, correct and ordain the future and save them from disappointment, and he laughed, thinking of the blackness that welled out of these men after each race, after each loss, the acceptance of disappointment, the yearning for pity, and yet there was a resilience, too, and a courage, the resiliency his mother had shown playing double solitaire.

Crede, standing on the clubhouse floor among these men, heard two of them agree that the favourite, the 6 horse, was going to win. He said out loud, "Only dead fish swim with the current," and a wiry little man who was known as Eli the Bat said, "Welcome to the fish market." There was tight-lipped grim laughter. Still, Crede knew that there was something luxurious to be felt in even the smallest win, a glee, and Crede believed he was going to win: *You think you're dead in the water and suddenly you're afloat and it's like a blessing, I can see that, a confirmation of oneself.* He made his bets without hesitation but none of his hunches fell into place. He swallowed hard when he lost the third race by a neck.

All that evening, as the track became an oval of light suspended in a vast darkness, he had to fight off an increasing sadness as, inexplicably, he lost race after race – and yet with each loss he also felt a desperate eagerness, a determination to keep on playing in antic-ipation of a win until – at a point in the ninth race, he suddenly leapt to his feet, ready to lose, yet throwing his hands into the air as the horses lunged around the turn into the stretch, unable to stop himself from yelling as the horses pounded toward the wire, and then, when the numbers of the first three horses crossed the wire, he could hardly believe what he knew to be true – there were his three numbers, three numbers that he had bet, and as he stood there, alone, flooded with a feeling of affirmation, as if some truth deep within himself had been confirmed, he could see the winning horses set in a stillness apart from the rest of the field as they had crossed the wire, and it was as though they had been positioned there at the wire at the beginning of the race, foreordained, and it was as if he had tapped into the order of things, as if life were not just caprice and consternation played close to the vest but life could be a moment of long shots, too.

The payoff for the Triple would be enormous, and he gave a little pump of his fist, but then he sat down in sullen wonder and put his fist up to his mouth, muffling his voice as he said, "Shit," suddenly suffering a chill. The Inquiry sign had come on, the thin red neon letters: INQUIRY. His father's favourite word. An inquiry had been called. Under his breath he cursed the stewards and hurried downstairs to the clubhouse floor to stand among other shuffling men who were watching the replay on the television monitor, and they reran the horses coming out of the gate from three angles, and it was clear to Crede before the decision was announced that his number 4 horse had bumped with the 5, taking the 5 out at the beginning, coming out of the gate and veering into him. It didn't matter that the 4 would have won anyway, or that the 5, at 30 to 1, had no chance – the 4 horse had accidentally interfered. He said aloud to himself: "It doesn't matter," but someone close by snarled, "Goddamn right it matters," because the stewards took the 4 horse down, and though he had won, he had lost. He was disqualified. "Just a minor detail, man," Eli the Bat said bitterly, and Crede suddenly screamed, "I'll fucking detail you, you bastards," surprising the other men who were used to disappointment as he hurried out of the clubhouse filled with outrage, as if, worse than being cheated, he had been taunted and mocked by a promise unkept. "Fucking jockey probably went in the tank." He drove home.

❊   ❊   ❊

When he came to the house, marching across the lawn and cutting through a flower bed, he tracked wet garden dirt through the front door and along the hall and up the unlit stairs. Filled with a desperate eagerness, a desperate anticipation – just as he had been ready to lose as the winning horses had come to the wire – he stood holding his breath outside his father's closed bedroom door, listening to laughter and little whelps *like goddamn puppy love, lapping it up,* and suddenly the dark stairwell seemed like a vast hole he and his father had lived in and shared and gone up and down in each day, elbows flared to ensure breathing space, and as he opened the door and crossed the line of the threshold to the dimly lit bedroom, that forbidden place from his childhood, a place of whisperings and broken breathing, in which the naked woman spun up and around and over his father, her hands held out, he suddenly felt a terrible sense of exhaustion and wanted to cry out some word of helpless remorse in his anger so that his father would understand that a cry at least could fill the emptiness that had been be-tween them since childhood, but then, seeing Grace's breasts and his bewildered father struggling, ungainly and sprawling under her in his marriage bed, Crede yelled, "You horse's ass."

Grace, seeing who it was, sank back against the propped pillows and smiled. "Welcome to the scene of the crime," she said, putting her hand lightly on the old man's shoulder, but the old man screamed, "What? You sonofabitch." Crede, rocking on the balls of his feet, unsure of what he was going to do, stared at the white

hair on his father's chest, *White for Chrissake as a lamb,*
and his skin hanging, his whole life hanging loose off his
bones like he was dried out in the wind, and Crede suddenly wanted to reach out and cradle the old man and
rock him, as if he were a shrivelled child, but his father,
as if slowly recollecting a rage, said, "You sonofabitch,
you sonofabitch, you come in on me naked, you dare,"
and he jackknifed up off the bed, both fists punching
the air, and as he fell back onto the sheet, Crede, who'd
spun away astonished, said, "Jesus," and when Grace
leapt off the bed, landing in a crouch, he laughed, but
then they both heard the rattle in the old man's throat
and stared at the gaping mouth, the wide eyes, and saw
that his father was dying, if not already dead. "I didn't
ask for any of this," Crede said, shaken, his eyes filling
with tears as he drew the woman to him, holding her
hard by the wrists. "I didn't want this."

"No, no, of course not," she said. She drew her hands
together so that they seemed to be caught in prayer.

❊   ❊   ❊

For the funeral in the cathedral, motorcycle policemen
wearing white crash helmets with plastic visors directed
traffic and despite a freak early snowstorm, heavy and
wet, an overflow of mourners clustered outside on the

steps of the cathedral. The mayor was there and sena-
tors and the deputy prime minister. A judge and the city
director of roads were among the pallbearers.

Crede walked down the centre aisle beside the bur-
nished oak casket that had been mounted on an alu-
minium rolling caisson, the casket covered with calla
lilies, and then he stepped into the front pew. The choir
sang the *Kyrie*. The priest, an aged man with strong
cheekbones and alert eyes in pouches of pale flesh, went
up into the pulpit and read from a prepared text, prais-
ing what he called his father's rare fidelity, that "uncom-
mon bond to the common weal, that duty to oneself –
such fidelity being a belief that can become a beatitude,"
he said, "because this fidelity is a good life so arranged
that it melds into all our lives . . . this fidelity, the virtue
of the good soldier, leads us onward as intimates as we
embrace each other in the shadow of death."

Then, after the *Credo,* the priest raised his hand and
made a sign of the cross, then motioned to Crede, who
stepped alongside the coffin and placed both hands on
the dark shining wood and sang, all alone, by special
dispensation, because it was not a Catholic hymn:

> *Amazing Grace, how sweet the sound,*
> *That saved a wretch like me;*
> *I once was lost but now am found . . .*

As Crede walked down the aisle behind the coffin, he nodded with the stern assurance of the deeply aggrieved to men and women he did not know, nodded as if they were old friends, or if not friends, then neighbours. He let people shake his hand and he stood on the curb beside the hearse, stroking his smooth cheek with his long fingers. The wet cold wind carried heavy flakes of snow that melted on his face and bare head, snow that refreshed him. Water trickled out of his hair, down his brow. He thought he caught a glimpse of Grace wearing a veil, making her way toward him between men and women bundled up against the wind and snow, clustered into small groups. *And it's just like the track*, he thought, *clustering for comfort,* and several well-dressed women reached out and offered their condolences.

After riding out to the burial yard, past the Chick 'n' Deli and U-Haul and Koko the Muffler King, the several limousines eased to a stop near an open grave. Surprisingly few mourners had actually come out to the grave, among them, two women he'd never seen before, both young and quite beautiful, standing apart and apparently a little perplexed by each other's presence. After a shovelful of dirt had been cast into the grave, Senator Mulroney took Crede's hand in his and said, "Your father was a man of means who always meant well."

"Yes, yes, he was well-meant," Crede said, and when Senator Mulroney looked puzzled, he said: "That's what they say about a horse who tried really hard but finished last." He turned away toward Grace who had stepped out from between two grey turreted tombstones.

"Well, Grace," he said, "how are you?"

"Never mind me," she said. "How are you?"

She held out her gloved hand and he shook it and saw that she was wearing a silver bracelet, inlaid with amethysts, that had belonged to his mother.

"Well, everything went as he would have wanted," he said, "and he'd be relieved."

"Your father would've liked all the arrangements."

"Yes, if he hadn't been a lawyer he'd have been a flower arranger."

"Now, now. I thought you sang beautifully," she said.

"Thank you. But if he'd had his way he would have brought his lawnmower to church."

"Lawnmower?"

"Never mind, private joke."

He looked down at her little ankle rubbers as she stood in the snow, and he laughed. "You should have boots," he said. "I'm surprised my father didn't buy you some boots," and he took her arm, helping her as they stepped around the small polished marble modern stones that were laid flat in the ground, some lost under the snow. "I think it's terrible," he said, "the way they won't let us put up real tombstones any more."

"They're so expensive, though," she said, "and such a waste of real money."

"But each tombstone's like a story," he said, "a little story we leave behind about our lives. It's terrible that he's just going to have an ordinary marker – Eldon Creed – like a little headline in a local newssheet – like he was nobody."

"He certainly wasn't a nobody," she said, as they turned along the lane toward the lead limousine.

"It was awfully good of you to come," he said. She lit a Nat Sherman cigarette.

A gust of wind lifted loose snow over the tombs and a lone skier suddenly appeared gliding between Dutch elm trees, poling over a rise and down around a tall cylindrical black monument.

"Jesus," he said, "a cross-country skier."

"Now, I've seen everything," she said.

The skier, wearing a white suit and goggles, coasted down an incline, swooped around a russet marble slab, and then poled past the small domed crematorium.

"I'll be damned," he said, bewildered by a sudden remorse, bewildered by a recollection of how he had wounded his father, and for a moment he couldn't believe that his father was dead – that the *tock tock tock* had stopped and that he was standing there in the deep wet snow of the burial yard watching a lone cross-country skier, who looked like an arctic soldier, pass between the tombs, and close to tears he turned to Grace, gripping her arm.

"I didn't want to hurt him, you know, not at all."

"No, I'm sure you didn't."

"Anyway, to tell you the truth, I thought I'd die laughing when you said, 'Welcome to the scene of the crime.'"

"It was something my mother used to say."

"Your mother went in for crime?"

"No, no. She was very prim, very proper, and very poor. It was words she picked up from the movies, like you might pick up a cold."

He touched her gloved hand and she took off the glove as the driver opened the limousine's door. She touched his cheek. Crede helped her into the back seat and then stood looking off through the bare trees, looking at the trail of the arctic skier. "What are you looking for?" she asked.

"Nothing," he said, "it's just, for some reason I remembered my mother telling me that 'It's God who's a sneak. He's sneaking around in our lives.'" And then:

"She liked to talk about a necessary dignity. Anyway, I think you should go on alone. I need to walk."

He leaned into the limousine, toward the driver, and said, "Take the lady to wherever she needs to go."

He closed the door and walked away, going toward the other side of the burial yard, deliberately taking very deep breaths, opening his lungs to the crispness on the air, realizing that by the time he got out to Yonge Street and hailed a taxi, his own shoes would be ruined, he would be soaking wet from the slush, and he would probably have caught a cold.

❄   ❄   ❄

At home in the empty house, soaked to the skin, he stood in the hollow of the stairwell, shivering.

"Ain't life a bitch," he said. And then: "Sorry, Mom."

He went upstairs to his bathroom, stripped off his clothes, and stepped into the shower stall, twisting the shower head to massage so that the pelting water would loosen his neck muscles, cranking the temperature dial to HOT, not just to burn the chill out of his bones but to steam himself clean of the glad-handing at the funeral Mass, the perfunctory piety displayed at the grave, and of Grace, who had expected him to want her.

After he showered, he put on his white terry-cloth bathrobe with the shawl collar and he stood in front of the bathroom wall mirror, drawing a large C into the steamed glass, and then he watched as a tear slowly formed on the glass and slid down through the C, leaving a trail glistening with mirrored light, like scar tissue, he thought.

"A mother knows when a boy is naked," he heard his mother say, as he ran his tongue along the quick of his forefinger, the cut almost healed.

At last, the steam disappeared, leaving a ghost of a C on the glass.

Though he had shaved at seven in the morning, he shaved again – drawing the straight blade back and down his jaw and neck – till he was satisfied by the suppleness of his skin to the touch of his long fingers, and then, as if it were necessary for him to actually hear himself say words about his father that he had kept to himself: "You fucking backstroker, all your life you were swimming on your back, belly-up, swimming with the current, a dead fish," and he sang out,

> The harder they come,
> the harder they fall,
> one and all . . .

His robe fell open. He was standing straight up. He stepped back from himself in the mirror, startled again by his pale skin and how dark his crotch hair was, but in the mirror light he saw that he was not lost in that darkness. He felt a rush of exhilaration.

"It's in the blood," he said. "It's in the blood."

DOG DAYS OF LOVE

Father Vernon Wilson was an old priest who led a quiet life. He said Mass every morning at the side altar of his church, read a short detective novel, had a light lunch, and went out walking with his dog. He was retired but he always made a few house calls to talk to old friends who weren't bothered by the dog, and though he had a special devotion to the Blessed Virgin and the Holy Shroud of Turin, he didn't talk much about faith.

Though he was still spry for a man in his early eighties, he gladly let the dog, a three-year-old golden retriever, set a leisurely pace on a loosely held leash, sniffing at curbs and shrub roots and fence posts. He'd had the dog for a year, a local veterinarian having come around to the parish house of an afternoon to leave the dog as a gift, telling the housekeeper, "I've always wanted to give Father Wilson a little dog. I always felt so at ease with myself and the world whenever I'd gone to him to confession."

In all his years as a parish priest, Father Wilson had never imagined that he might want a dog, and he certainly did not know if he could, in accordance with diocesan rules, keep a dog in the parish home. The new young pastor, Father Kukic, had at first said, No, no, he wasn't sure that it was a good idea at all, even if it was possible, but then the diocesan doctor had come by to give the priests their autumn flu shots and to check their blood pressure, and he had said, "No, no, it's a wonderful idea, I urge you, Father Kukic, if it's not usually done, to do it. It's a proven fact, older people who have the constant company of a dog live longer, maybe five years longer, maybe because all a dog asks is that you let him love you, and we all want Father Wilson to live longer, don't we."

"I'm sure we do," Father Wilson said.

"Well," Father Kukic said, trying to be amiably amusing, "there could be two sides to that argument."

"Father Kukic," the old priest said, feigning surprise, "I've never known you to see two sides to an argument." He clapped the young priest on the shoulder. "Good for you, good for you."

"I'm sure, too, that the dog will be good for you," Father Kukic said.

"I'm sure he will," Father Wilson said, but he was not sure of the situation at all. On their first night walk together he kept the dog on a short leash, calling him simply, "You, dog . . . ."

Then, after ten or eleven days, Father Wilson not only let the dog sleep on the floor at the end of the bed in his room, but sometimes up on the end of his bed, and then one morning he announced over breakfast that he had decided to call the dog, Anselm. "After the great old saint," he told Father Kukic, "Saint Anselm, who said the flesh is a dung hill, and this dog, I can tell you, has yet to meet doggy dung on a lawn he doesn't like."

"Oh, really now," Father Kukic said, and before he could add anything more, the old priest said, "But then, look at it this way, nothing is ever what it seems. Most people get Saint Anselm all wrong. He was like the great hermit saints who went out into the desert, they renounced everything that gave off the smell of punishment and revenge, and so they renounced the flesh, but only so they could insist on the primacy of love over everything else in their spiritual lives . . . over knowledge, solitude, over prayer . . . love, in which all authoritarian brutality and condescension is absent, love in which nothing is to be hidden in the flesh . . . ."

Father Kukic sat staring at him, breathing through his open mouth.

"You should be keeping up on your spiritual reading, Father, that's Thomas Merton I was giving you there, you should try him."

"Wasn't he something of a mystic?"

"My goodness," the old priest said, "I think Anselm and I should go for a walk, get our morning feet on the ground."

They walked together every morning just before lunch, sometimes in the afternoon if it wasn't too hot or too cold, and always at night, just before *Larry King*. "If you're going to be in touch, if you're going to keep up with your parishioners," he told Father Kukic, "you've got to know what the trash talk is, too."

When he visited homes in the parish, leaving the dog leashed on a porch or sitting in a vestibule, he talked candidly about anything and everything, pleasing the parishioners, but more and more as he and Anselm walked together, and particularly when they stopped to rest for a moment in front of a building like the Robarts Research Library, he leaned down and patted Anselm's neck and said quietly to him, "Good dog, now you look at that, there's real brutalism for you, that's the bunker mentality of a bully." He scowled at the massive slab-grey concrete windowless wall, the cramped doorway under a huge periscope projection of concrete into the sky. "This is the triumph of the architecture of condescension," he said, pleased that he'd found so apt a phrase for his thought, and amused and touched, too, by how Anselm, looking up at him, listened attentively, and how the dog, at the moment he had finished his thought, came up off his haunches and broke into a cantering walk, striding, the old priest thought, like a small blond horse.

"Beautiful," he said, "beautiful."

Parishioners and shopkeepers soon took for granted seeing them together.

The only times that Anselm was not with him, the only time he left the dog alone in his bedroom, was when he said Mass at the side altar early in the morning or when he went to visit a parishioner sick at home.

Once, while he was away on a sick call, Anselm had chewed the instep of a shoe he had left under the bed, and a week later he had swallowed a single black sock.

That had caused an awkward moment, because the dog had not been able to entirely pass the sock and Father Wilson had had to stand out on the parish-house lawn behind a tree and slowly drag the slime and shit-laden sock out of the dog.

"Anselm, my Anselm," he had said, "you sure are a creature of the flesh."

But it was while he was at prayer that he felt closest to Anselm.

It was while he knelt at prayer before going to bed, kneeling under the length of linen cloth that hung on the wall, a replica of the Holy Shroud of Turin, that Anselm had sat down beside him and had nestled his body in under his elbow so that the old priest had embraced Anselm with his right arm as he had said the Apostles Creed, feeling deeply, through the image of the dead face on the Shroud, the Presence of the Living Christ in his life and now, every night, they knelt and sat together for ten minutes, after which Father Wilson would cross himself, get into bed, and Anselm would leap up on to the bed and curl at his feet so that as he went to sleep, the old priest was comforted not just by the heat and weight of the animal in his bed, but the sound of his breathing.

His devotion to the Shroud, however, had not been a comfort to his young pastor, Father Kukic, who had snorted dismissively, saying that when a seminarian in Paris he had travelled through the countryside one summer, and as a believer, about to be ordained, he had been embarrassed to come upon a church near Poitiers that had claimed to house "one of the two known heads of John the Baptist," and another that had said they possessed "a vial of the unsoured milk of the Virgin."

"The unsoured milk . . . . I like that," the old priest had said, laughing.

"Well, I don't, and no one else does either," Father Kukic said. "It's embarrassing."

"Only a little."

"And as for your cloth, no one had ever heard of your Shroud til somewhere back in the 1500s."

"Not mine, Father. Our Lord's."

"Oh please."

"The thing is this, Father, there are certain facts," and Father Wilson had patiently tried to describe the two images on the Shroud – the front and back of a man's wounded body and his bearded face, his staring eyes and skeletal crossed hands – and how all this, after experts had completed a microscopic examination of the linen, had revealed no paint or pigment that anyone knew of, nor did the image relate to any known style . . . and furthermore, "Somehow, the Shroud is a kind of photographic negative which becomes positive when reversed by a camera, the body of a man somehow embedded in the linen as only a camera can see him, a way of observing what no one could have known how to possibly paint."

"These all may be facts, Father, but they prove nothing."

"Exactly, my dear Father. But you see, I prefer that facts add up to a mystery that is true rather than facts that add up to an explanation that is true."

"Like what?"

"Like the Virgin Birth."

"Nonsense. That's a matter of faith."

"No, it's a matter of temperament, Father."

They had never spoken of the Shroud again.

There were nights through the winter when the old priest, before going to sleep, had felt, as he had told Anselm, "nicely confused." Kneeling under the Shroud, knowing how dark and freezing cold it was outside and staring up into the hollowed dead yet terrorized eyes of the Christ, he had felt only warmth and unconditional love from the dog under his arm, and after saying his prayers he had taken to nestling his face into Anselm's neck fur, laughing quietly and boyishly, as he hadn't heard himself laugh in years, before falling into a very sound sleep.

At the first smell of spring, he opened his bedroom window and aired out his dresser drawers and his closet, breathing in deeply and deeply pleased to be alive. He gave Anselm's head a brisk rubbing and then, having borrowed the housekeeper's feather duster, he took down the linen shroud that had been brought to him as a gift by a friend all the way from Turin, and he dusted it off at the window and then laid it out for airing over the sill, as his mother had done years ago with the family bedsheets.

In the early afternoon, leaving Anselm asleep, he went out alone to visit an elderly couple whose age and infirmness over the long winter had made them cranky and curt and finally cruel to each other, though they still loved each other very much, and he hoped that they would let him, as an old friend, go around their flat and open their windows, too, and bring the feel of the promise of spring air into their lives again.

When he returned to the parish house, to his room, he was exuberant, enormously pleased with himself, because his visit had ended with the elderly couple embracing him, saying, "We're just three old codgers waiting to die," laughing happily.

When he opened his door, he let out a roar of disbelief, "Nooooo, God." Anselm was on his belly on the bed and under him – gathered between his big web-toed paws – was the Shroud. He was thumping his tail as he snuffled and shoved his snout into the torn cloth. The old priest lunged, grabbing for the Shroud, yanking at it, the weight of the startled dog tearing it more, and when he saw, in disbelief, that the face, the Holy face and the Holy eyes of the Presence were all gone, shredded and swallowed by the dog, he raised his fist – hurt and enraged – and Anselm, seeing that rage and that fist, leaped off the bed, hitting the floor, tail between his legs, skidding into a corner wall where, cowering and trembling, trying to tuck his head into his shoulder, he looked up, waiting to be beaten.

"Oh my God, oh my God," the old priest moaned, sitting on the edge of the bed, drawing the ruined Shroud across his knees.

He could not believe the look of terror, and at the same time, the look of complete love in the dog's eyes, and for a moment he thought that that must have been the real look in Christ's eyes as He hung on the cross, His terror felt as a man, and His complete unconditional love as God, but before he could wonder if such a thought was blasphemous, he was struck by a fear that, having seen his rage and his fist, Anselm would always be afraid of him, would always cower and tremble at his coming. As a boy, he had seen dogs like that, dogs who had been beaten.

He fell on to his knees beside the dog in the corner where, night after night, he had prayed – saying the Apostles Creed, affirming his faith – and Anselm had sat there, too, waiting to go on to the bed to sleep. He took Anselm's head in his arms, feeling as he did his trouser leg become warm with an oily wetness, the dog, in the confusion of his fear and relief at being held, having peed. The old priest hugged him closer and laughed and Anselm came out of his cower and then stopped trembling. Rocking Anselm in his arms, he was about to tell him he was a good dog and he shouldn't worry, that he loved him, but then he thought how ludicrous it would be for a grown man to talk out loud to a dog about something so serious as love, and so he just sat in their wetness holding Anselm even tighter so that Anselm would understand and never doubt.

PAUL VALÉRY'S SHOE

I have tried as hard as I can to tell stories, not necessarily what I'd call true stories, but stories that have a true feel to their ending, true to how I feel in my heart. What happens is that I start a story with a particular face, a particular phrase, and soon thereafter I have a page or two – or ten or twelve – but coming to where the story has to end the only thing that ends is my knowing what more there is to say. I sit staring at the dance of dust in the light. Sometimes I'll keep typing, searching for that shoe that Paul Valéry said is out there waiting for the story that's true to itself, the perfect fit. But no matter how bold my start has been, soon there's nothing more to say and I end up shelved in my own head. So the hours pass and I try to peck out a line, a paragraph, I keep trying to look for the ending back in the beginning. I refuse to take the easy way out of a story. A clean resolution is no more an option than the death of the main character – those are not endings, they're just death, tidiness. That's just having absolutely nothing to say. So what do I do, caught between nothing to say and no ending because I don't understand my beginning? I sit here in this room with these ridiculous old curtains on the window, curtains that remind me of my childhood because they are worked with an appliqué of the letters of the alphabet, the promise that the alphabet is, and I am sitting in this dark room lit only by a lamp on the night table with the stand-up mirror on the table, trying to tell this particular story about a writer who is actually starving to death while he is writing the story of how he is eating himself alive – refusing under any circumstances to quit on himself or his story because he is too much of an optimist, as all storytellers have to be optimists, because they believe that there is that shoe out there that fits – they can't help themselves from starting a new story because they know that somewhere in the beginning there is an end – as I believe that there has to be an end even for this tawdry, shameful story that I'm trying to write – a story as cramped as these two tiny rooms where I sit and catch inadvertently an appalling glimpse of my sneaky little face in the bedside mirror, the face of a dolt sneering back at me – sneering because that dolt knows that I still believe the phrase "a petal falls" is a touching, moving phrase – sneering at me, his eyes shining bright in the gloom, as I'm sure my own eyes are shining, the eyes of a starving man, chewing like an anxious girl on my knuckle, too stupid to feel pain, and then chewing on another knuckle, as if coming to an agreement with that dolt about a phrase could save me, could spring open the light that is in all the little phrases I have hidden away in notebooks – the lines of conversation overheard and written down, lines so quick and easy to whoever said them, quick as the curl of a lip, quick as an eye dropped in sleep, all, all of them, the words, seeming at first as fresh and alive as fireflies at night but turning to ash in the morning, ashes in the mouth whenever I've sat here like I'm sitting here now, day-after-day, TAP TAP on the keys, hearing "a petal falls" – "a petal falls," not eating for nine days now – stroking my wrists, stroking the mildew-like tracing of my own veins in the skin, so delicate, not believing that any of what is now happening is true. I mean, could I actually die of hunger, die out of want for a story, die at the only point in my storytelling life where I actually have an ending, die because in fact I have ab-solutely nothing left of myself, I mean, could I actually end by eating my own heart out? Could I end up, after more pages pile up and pass, being so light-headed from hunger and typing and licking between my tendons in this hour that is so cold that it takes my breath away, that I eat what is necessary, possible, getting down to the heart of who I am as I ease one word, and then another, into a shoe – a shoe that fits as I end my story, yes, end it by saying, yes, with utter storytelling simplicity, yes, how much I hate the words, "Once upon a time . . . ."

WITHOUT SHAME

*One thing alone is more tragic than suffering,
and that is the life of a happy man.*

— ALBERT CAMUS

Alice Kopff and her brother, Lyle, owned a bakery shop.
He was thirty-six, she was thirty-three. He baked the
breads. She was the pastry chef, a pale, plain woman
who was so constantly bright-eyed and ebullient that
Lyle said, "Sometimes I think you must be one of those
happiness flashers for Jesus."

"Not likely," she laughed.

"But even after the funeral . . . ."

Two years earlier, their mother and father, who had
opened the Kopff & Kopff Bakery Shoppe after coming
to Toronto from Dresden, had died of smoke inhala-
tion. A fire that had broken out behind the ovens had
crawled quickly across the floor, trapping them in the

kitchen. They had suffered severe burns to the face. Their coffins had been closed. During the funeral mass, Lyle, arms folded, holding on to himself, had said, "It is incredible to me that our mother and father who, as youngsters, survived the wartime firestorming of Dresden, who had then made of their life . . . not fire but bread . . . should here, among us, nonetheless die of fire . . . ."

Alice, veiled and dressed in black, had wept in her pew as if she were inconsolable, yet after the service, standing out in sunlight on the church porch, she had lifted her veil, and had looked delighted as she took hold of every hand extended to her. Lyle thought she had lost her mind.

The eager young parish priest, Father Dowd, was disarmed by what he thought was her avoidance of the vanities of grief, and whispered to her, "I'm glad that you . . . ."

"Yes," she'd called out, "a gladness . . . ."

That night, over a supper of cold meats, Lyle had asked, "What came over you . . . ?"

"Nothing."

"What do you mean, nothing?"

"Nothing. Nothing's nothing."

"No it's not."

"Yes it is, plain and simple."

"I just wondered," he had said mournfully, "how, with both mother and father fresh in the ground, you could be so happy?"

Crossing her knife and fork on her plate, she said:

> As I was going out one day
> My head fell off and rolled away.
> When I saw that it was gone
> I picked it up and put it on.

❈   ❈   ❈

Then, she got pregnant. No one knew who the father was. She would give no name. Lyle was furious. "The shame." He pounded the granite countertop beside the cash register with his fist: "This is a complete betrayal of everything Mother and Father stood for."

"Maybe."

"Maybe what?"

"Maybe not."

"Maybe yes. And who'll look after the child?"

"There'll be no problem," she said.

She bought an old black wicker pram at a thrift store. She wheeled it, full of freshly cut flowers, up and down the street, to and from the shop.

"I think I'll call the child Happy," she said. "If it's a girl, she can be a dancer, and if it's a boy, he can play second base for the Yankees – Happy Kopff at second base."

"Happy's not a name," Lyle said.

"You could try being happy yourself," she said.

"I am happy. Who says I'm not? However, I'm no fool."

"Meaning I am." she said.

She folded her hands across her stomach, and then with a pouting, playful little smile, she said again, "There'll be no problem."

"Of course there's a problem."

"No there's not."

"It's awful, it really is, you're without shame."

When she told Father Dowd that she was pregnant, but there was no problem, he said, "No, no, there is certainly a problem, a problem that requires at least some regret, some weeping."

"You mean confession?"

"At least."

She said she would not go to confession, for she didn't like confession, but promised Father Dowd that she would say an Act of Contrition alone in her room. "I'll put penance to bed with me," she said, smiling. And for four days she went without lunch and for four days she did not put flowers in the pram, and, when she said hello to neighbours passing in the street or to customers in the shop, she did so with a contrite pout, but then one morning she appeared at the shop with a little red tear painted under each of her eyes, like a doll's tears, and she stood in the shop kitchen delighted to be laughing again, through her painted tears, tears that by the end of the day, because of the intense heat from the ovens, had run in streaks down her cheeks.

"You look goddam insane," Lyle said.

She shrugged and said, "Don't be silly, I'm happy as a lark," and she turned on the radio to listen to the baseball game while she worked. On the way home she bought two large bouquets of flowers for the black wicker pram. She did not, however, wheel it up and down the street. "That'll come soon enough," she said.

When she was taken to hospital and went into labour, she was three weeks early. It was a breech birth, the boy child coming out feet first, dead.

She overheard Father Dowd say to Lyle, "The child's soul has gone to limbo."

At the undertaker's, she told the priest, "He's right here in my heart. My heart's alive in him."

One week after the burial, she came into the bakery in the morning, her long hair tied in a single thick braid. She was wearing a smock that was baby blue. She said she was going to come to work wearing her baby-blue smock every day, like she was going to wear her tears. She laughed a shy little laugh. Lyle said sternly, "Why not wear normal white? Wipe the slate clean."

By closing hour at the end of that week, when the kitchen and counter staff were convinced she was going to be as easy-going and cheerful as ever, as Lyle stood with his arms buried up to his elbows in a vat of flour, they circled around her and rapped their pastry brushes, spoons, and even a rolling pin on the granite counter and gave her a clap of hands.

She was so moved by the applause that she untied her braid, letting her hair hang loose, and then, once she was at home she wheeled the pram out to the centre of the front lawn and filled it with potting earth. The next day she bought and planted an ornamental dwarf pine – "a pine that will grow green all year" – and she surrounded the fingerling branches of the pine with red and white impatiens.

"The colours of the resurrection," Father Dowd said, trying to cheer Lyle up.

"The pram's morbid," Lyle said.

"A touch, it is that, perhaps," the young priest said.

"Morbid," he told Alice.

"Not at all," Alice said. "Everything can be made to be happy," and then she broke into a grin, with her hands on her hips, as if she were challenging him.

He said nothing. But he told Father Dowd, "I think she's maybe hysterical."

Father Dowd said, "I don't know, perhaps something quite profound is at work in her, not just the acceptance of God's will, but out of the darkness, out of the sin and death that was the birth, has come the renewal of a joy that is inherent in death. It is the mystery of the Cross, is it not?"

That weekend, on the feast of Corpus Christi, Alice baked a five-layer chocolate-mocha cake for the priests at the parish church of the Blessed Sacrament. She carried the cake in a white cardboard box to the parish house. Father Dowd, standing in slippers at the door, said he would offer a special prayer of thanksgiving for her at Mass.

"For my child, too," she said.

"Of course, and if there's any need, any emergency, you call me."

"Life is an emergency," she said, eyes bright.

❊   ❊   ❊

A few weeks later, she had the shop delivery man carry five cakes to the Knights of Columbus church basement Friday night supper. After some confusion, the Knight Exemplar, realizing the cakes were a gift from Kopff and

Kopff, doffed his plumed hat, and happily ordered that the cakes be carried to the kitchen for cutting.

"Isn't Alice Kopff a Christian to contend with," the Knight Exemplar said to his fellow knights, as coffee and her cakes were served.

"Isn't Kopff a German-Jewish name, the two *ff*s?" one of the Knights asked.

"As far as I know she's completely Catholic."

"Not that it matters."

As the Knights seated in the round, ten to each table, discovered coins in their cake and cleared icing away from their prizes, the Knight Exemplar, moved, said, "I have always liked to think that we men, as Knights in the army of our Lord, have not lost a sense of where we come from, that God's dirt is under our nails. But suddenly I realize what it is that some of us have lost, and that is – the delight at finding a penny in our cakes, the delight that a child knows in discovering there are grace moments in life . . . ."

"Alice is a wonder," Father Dowd said, and after Sunday Mass, as Lyle waited for her in the emptied church, he thanked her from the altar for what he called her "generosity, her infectious irrepressible lightness of spirit," smiling down at her as she, seated alone in the pew that had become her usual place at Mass, smiled up at him.

"I think I might go to confession," she said.

Over lunch, Lyle said, "That priest, Father Dowd, he's got some kind of thing about you."

❊   ❊   ❊

On some nights, particularly weekend nights after they had worked hard all day in the heat of the kitchen, Lyle heard – after supper – what he thought were moans from her bedroom, and he was sure that she was talking to herself. He couldn't tell by her tone, as he stood at the bottom of the stairs, whether she was angry or not – or, perhaps she was praying, but he gave no thought to going silently up the stairs to listen: that would have been an invasive intimacy, and he shied away from any intimacies if he could (there had been women in his life but he'd liked best those who had expected the least from him). He stayed at the bottom of the stairs. Her moans sounded almost sexual, or, like she was in pain, yet there was certainly no one with her in her room (he'd spent several hours, off and on, wondering where, in what room, she had bedded down with an unknown man, and when – and for how long? When had she been out of his sight, and could it have possibly been in her own room – under his eye, so to speak – without him seeing? The possibility filled him with panic; could he, in his own house have had no idea of what was going on?). Rattled, he didn't know what to think, especially in the morning when she appeared for her toast and coffee looking well-slept, refreshed, with no clouding of sleeplessness or pain in her eyes.

"I must remember to water the flowers in the pram," she said. "My little dwarf pine."

"It looks ridiculous. It's not a pot."

"Then what is it?"

"It's not a flowerbed."

"It's a deathbed," she said firmly.

They divided the morning newspaper. He took the editorial section, she the sports page.

"The Leafs lost . . . ." she said.

"Oh yeah."

"In sudden-death," she said.

He put his page down: "We've never talked very much, have we?"

"You mean talking talk, or real talk? We've always talked talk, if we had to."

"Real talk," he said.

"Well, I wouldn't know what to say."

"No."

"Or why."

"No."

"Mother and Dad never seemed to need to talk very much."

"Yes. I always thought that that's what was so sane about them," he said. "I mean, they seemed, I don't know . . . ."

"Together."

"I suppose it's because of them I've always known it was okay to have nothing to say."

"We're kind of accomplices," she said.

"You mean the shop?"

"No. In solitude. We are accomplices in solitude."

He looked into her eyes, at her painted tears, and he said, "You know," laughing, an unguarded laugh that she had almost never heard from him, "sometimes I think you're out of your mind."

She laughed, too, her sprightly laugh and said, as if she needed to somehow reassure him, "If I'm out of my mind, it's all right with me."

❊   ❊   ❊

On Sundays, after the taking of communion, when the congregants turned to each other in their pews to shake hands, to embrace, she didn't notice – as she eagerly clasped hand after hand – that some parishioners, confronted by her relentless goodwill, shied away from her.

Father Dowd noticed, and he wondered – the next time she came to confession, and she was now coming once a week though she had little or nothing to confess – if he shouldn't try to speak to her about how dangerous candour is, how it does not bring out the best in most people but makes them feel inadequate, and he thought he should suggest that she be less effusive, less delighted by her own enthusiasms.

After Mass, however, out on the porch steps, when she took Father Dowd in a two-handed clasp, exuding all her open generosity of spirit, her seemingly guileless goodwill, he couldn't resist: he held her with two hands himself.

"More and more there is a gladness in my heart," she said, as she backed down the stairs, calling out, "and don't forget to pray for my son. He's not in limbo. I don't believe in limbo."

One of the other priests, Father McClure, after lunch, as if he were having an idle thought between pitches as they watched a baseball game on television, said, "You know, Father Dowd, I'm not sure we should encourage that woman, all that ridiculous gushing good feeling . . . . And those painted tears. Please . . . ."

Father Dowd didn't answer. Someone hit a home run for the Blue Jays and Father McClure stood up, clapping, enthusiastic.

❋   ❋   ❋

For the annual Field Day held in the gym at the parish school, Alice sent, by Kopff & Kopff delivery van, eight large icing-lathered cakes to the grade school home rooms – each of the cakes seeded with nickels, dimes, quarters, and one silver dollar. Lyle, as he banged his fists together in exasperation, told her, "This is not good. Not for you. Not for me. The expense, the expense to us out of pocket, and all the hours you take to make those cakes . . . ."

Seated at her work table, she was building a tall cone of chocolate profiteroles, each pastry ball filled with cream – "wiring" the balls together with spun caramel. "For a person like me, who is a pastry chef," she said, looking up at Lyle through filaments of caramel, gold in the light, "making a cake is as easy as falling down. Besides, I'm sure you've noticed that our business has probably tripled . . . the wives of the Knights of Columbus have done us no harm . . . ."

"For Christ's sake, they call you the Cake Lady."

"That's better than calling me a whore, which some did."

"And you think gladness of heart is a defence . . . ?"

"I don't think like you do, not at all. I don't need to defend myself. I'm guilty of nothing."

He sighed, opened the ovens, and went back to ladling mounds of dough into the fire, singing over and over a gay little ditty that was trapped in his mind: *I got plenty of nothing and nothing's got plenty for me . . . .*

He tried to find in his head another song to sing.

He couldn't.

None of this is fair, he thought, unsure of what was unfair as he stood among pleased customers who were lined up in front of the pastry showcases.

"Dessert is such a pleasure," he said to a woman, startling her as she waited by the cash register. "Isn't it?"

"Yes. Yes it is," she said defensively.

"Have a chocolate mousse tart," he blurted out, "on the house."

"Why, thank you, thank you. What an unexpected surprise."

"Yes," he said, and gave her a big smile, pleased with himself.

Several teachers at the parish school, however, were not pleased with Alice's cakes. They had not anticipated that several students, with more cake than they could eat, would start cake fights in the halls, lobbing gobs of icing against the walls, smearing cream across the chalkboards, fighting over the prize monies. And one irate mother complained that bigger boys had bullied all the quarters and silver dollars out of other children and had offered the money to her daughter if they could touch her bare breasts and she had let them touch her, and she had come home sick from too much cake and icing, her jeans pockets heavy with coins and her training bra lost behind the playground steel-link fencing.

No one told Alice about these children.

Many parents did not want her told. They said it was terrible, given her generosity, that she – who had asked for nothing in return – should be blamed for the evil inclinations of some unruly children. "It is unbelievable that a guileless spirit should be told to stop," one parent said at a meeting in the principal's office, "and told to stop with all the meanness we can muster."

❊   ❊   ❊

Lyle got up from the living-room sofa. He heard her moaning, a deep pulsing moan that he could not ignore. He stood at the bottom of the stairs, listening. He felt a chill come over him, something deep, a ground chill. He had cocked a cold eye on her that morning and he had been astonished to see how frail she was, her skin translucent, almost a glazed tint of blue beneath the skin. He realized that she had been eating less and less, looking more and more pleased the less she ate.

He undid the laces of his shoes and in his stocking feet went stealthily up the stairs to her bedroom door that was ajar. She was sitting naked in shadow light in a rocking chair. He could see that she was cradling a bundle of white in her arms, but he couldn't tell if the bundle was blankets, or whether the blankets contained a doll, and for a shuddering moment he thought, *What if it's the child?* knowing, since he had seen the boy in its tiny coffin, that it was not the child. She moaned again but she had, at the same time, such a contented look on her face, a look of such stillness and calm that he felt confused and ashamed for having, like a sneak in his own house, looked on her in her nakedness.

My God, he thought, hurrying downstairs, *I've seen her like she's never seen herself.*

❈   ❈   ❈

That week, a parent who was a lawyer announced to Father Dowd and the school principal, and then to the press, that his daughter – "a young girl having every expectation of becoming a successful teenage model" – had broken a front tooth on a penny in the Field Day cakes. At a small press conference on the school steps, he announced that he was suing the school and Alice Kopff for twenty-five thousand dollars. "I intended to be a model," the chubby girl whined, showing a gap in her mouth to a photographer from the *Sun.*

Confronted at the shop by two newsmen who had been sent by their papers to speak to her, Alice said simply, "I have done what I've done in memory of my own dead child."

"Is that why the painted tears?" a reporter asked, snickering. "And what was the child's name?"

"His name is a secret."

"And the father?"

"He's a secret, too. He doesn't matter. That we do good is what matters. That we do good. Any priest will tell you that."

"What about the lawyer, the twenty-five thousand?"

"I don't know about any of that."

The following day in the parish house, Father McClure slammed the *Sun* down on a table in front of Father Dowd.

"Do good," he cried, "do good! Any priest will *not* tell you that . . . ."

He was red in the face.

"Relax. Watch the baseball game."

"Baseball . . . do you realize what's going on, Father Dowd? There's upheaval in the classrooms, lawsuits, we're giving scandal to the church in the press, and we're here, you and me, yelling at each other . . . ."

"I don't know," Father Dowd said. "She only wishes well, she only wants people to be happy."

"Happy!" Father McClure said, almost sneering. "The message of the Cross is not happiness. Jesus did not die happy."

❖   ❖   ❖

It was the week of First Communion for the first grade students at the parish school. Alice worked late Thursday and Friday, working by herself at the big stainless steel oven. The heat in the kitchen was intense. *We could use more air,* she thought. There would be almost three-hundred parents and children at the Communion reception after Sunday Mass. Alice, going about her work, felt feverish and she knew that her face must be flushed because Lyle, before leaving the shop for home, had taken a long look at her – as if he thought he should caution her – but she had put her finger to her lips.

Then she had blown him a kiss and he had blushed.

On Sunday morning before the eleven o'clock Mass, the Kopff & Kopff van arrived at the side door to the reception hall. The delivery man carried in flat box after flat box stamped – COMMUNION CUPCAKES: five hundred little cakes in round fluted paper cups. She enclosed a handwritten note to Father Dowd, explaining that these cakes were not only an original recipe, but just before the mould trays had gone into the oven she had taken a wafer of white chocolate and pressed it in under the cap of each cake so that when the cakes were baked the wafers would melt, would transform completely and become the cake, white and unseen, while still being chocolate, which, as best as she could understand, was what happened at communion.

She wished him every happiness in Jesus.

The communion cupcakes were a huge success, not just with the children but with the parents, too.

Father McClure was apoplectic.

"This is outrageous, this diminution, this belittlement of the Blessed Sacrament . . . she has to stop, an end must be made of it."

Father Dowd reluctantly agreed and telephoned the Kopff house.

Lyle said that she had had a coffee with him, watered the flowers in the pram, and then had gone to the shop saying that she wanted to sit alone on that Sunday afternoon in the empty kitchen.

"She looked very happy, almost blissful," he told Father Dowd, who hurried to the shop, and finding the front door open, went in, hesitated, and then stepped around the cash register and counter into the kitchen.

"Welcome to the inner sanctum," she said.

She was sitting in front of the big oven.

"I have been so happy all morning," she said, "I'm so happy I could die. I could die and be happy with my little boy."

He hesitated, afraid that any admonition, any cautioning word would seem petty to her. He wanted to say something serious, but only as a warning of what to expect from Father McClure and others like him.

"Have a cupcake," she said.

"Not just now."

"Well, some white chocolate then," and she handed him a tray of white chocolate wafers. "I'd be very hurt if you didn't have one," she said.

He took a wafer, bit into it, and swallowed.

She closed her eyes. He licked a leftover sweetness from his lips.

"I call to mind," he said, almost in a whisper, "two lines of poetry I like very much . . . ."

"Yes . . . I like poetry, too," she said, smiling, eyes still closed.

"So do I," he said.

Then he said softly,

A perfect paralyzing bliss
Contented as despair.

Folding her hands, she said, "I don't know what that means."

"Well, perhaps neither do I. It's hard to know the meaning of what we say or do."

"All I know is that everything means more than we think it does," she said.

"I suppose," he said. "I suppose that's true. Though my friend, Father McClure, likes to say that all of this means less than meets the eye."

"I spy with my little eye," she said, opening one eye, and giggling.

"Yes," he said.

"That's what I've always liked about you," she said.

"What?"

"There are people who say yes and people who say no. You nearly always say yes. Mind you, I said yes once and look where it got me."

"Where's that?"

"Pregnant." She laughed and took a wafer of white chocolate herself.

"And ever since, I've learned to live with death being alive in me."

He lowered his eyes for a moment. Then, he almost whispered when he said, "About the communion cup-cakes . . . ."

"The idea was so simple," she said.

"Yes, I guess it was."

"I guess so."

"Well . . . ." and resenting Father McClure, his sneering tone, he stood up, saying, "I must go . . . tickets for the baseball game, a 1:30 start, a kind parishioner gave me tickets for the Blue Jays game . . . ."

"That," she said, standing up to shake his hand, "was my dream, you know."

"What?"

"That my boy would play second base for the Yankees. Happy Kopff at second base . . . ."

He felt not only a sorrow for her, but something harder, the loss of something he'd never had a chance to have.

He stepped out of the shop into the relief of afternoon sunlight.

❊   ❊   ❊

Father McClure heard the nearby sirens in the parish house. He put his stole around his neck, ready for the worst, and hurried after the fire trucks.

Father Dowd, at the baseball game, was unhappy: the score was 3-2 for the Yankees.

Father McClure gave the last rites to dead Alice in the back of an ambulance. Father Dowd came home, pleased because the Blue Jays had beaten the Yankees in extra innings, 4-3.

❊   ❊   ❊

"Our estimate," the Fire Chief said to the press, "is that somewhere between 1:30 and 2:00, a fairly rare, but known form of spontaneous combustion occurred – the technical name is pyrolysis, the transformation of a compound in dried-out old wood that is caused by heat. It seems the old wood over the big oven just burst into flames. You might recall the same thing happened in Perl's Kosher Deli on Bathurst Street last year. She didn't have a chance, the whole place went up in flames in no time flat."

The funeral Mass at Blessed Sacrament was said by Father McClure. It was so crowded, with children especially, that latecomers had to stand on the church steps. In the pulpit, Father Dowd spoke of Alice's unblemished goodwill and how the goodness of spirit can be infectious just as her mysterious generosity of spirit – born out of great loss but unsoured by loss – had been infectious in the community. Many in the pews wept as he lamented her passing: "She was so much on the side of life."

Standing by the black limousine that was about to carry her coffin to the burial yard, Lyle thanked Father Dowd and said, "You know, what's a mystery to me is that my family has been in one firestorm after another, first in Dresden, then my mother and father dying by fire, and now this. Alice up in flames."

"Well, no, I hadn't thought of that," Father Dowd said. "There seems to be so much I haven't thought about her. I have the feeling I may have let her down."

"Maybe."

Lyle wryly laughed so loudly that Father Dowd looked at him with concern.

"Maybe," he said, "it'll be me in the fire next time."

That evening, Lyle transplanted the dwarf pine out of the black wicker pram to the lawn, kneading the earth around the root. Then he emptied out all of the potting earth and put the pram at the curb for the garbage pick-up in the morning.

He remained inside the house for a week. One night he thought he heard her moaning in her room and he went to stand at the bottom of the stairs, even though he knew that she was not there. A second time, he blew her a kiss. "I owed you one," he whispered. He saw no one for the week, not until the estate lawyer knocked on the door.

Over coffee and afternoon bitters, the lawyer explained that Alice's will, though very simple, was complicated.

She had willed all her goods and possessions – a substantial account at the bank, her half-interest in

Kopff & Kopff the Bakery Shoppe, all her recipes, and her half-interest in the family house – to her dead child, Happy Kopff.

"Happy . . . ."

"Don't worry," the lawyer said, "it's complicated, but we'll unravel whatever she's done."

SEWING

After the shelling, under a cloudy sky and on the out-skirts of the town of Bibić, they drove past the caved-in roofs of farmhouses, entering a road that was empty, except for a cowering pariah dog and an old woman who was sitting on a red kitchen chair by the side of the road, sitting in a nest of black shawls in front of a burned-out shop. There were six or seven old foot-pedal sewing machines in front of the shop.

"Where's everybody?"

"Our sons, they're gone, they were the seamstresses who worked those machines," the old woman said. "Soldiers coming through the valley wanted to know which of our seamstresses was the poet and when the boys refused to speak up, a man in the militia sewed their mouths shut."

"Did your sons say who did it, which side the mili-tia was on?"

"Their lips are sealed."

THE VENTRILOQUIST

His name was Thom. He came from a family of black preachers and ventriloquists, men and women able to throw their voices, some from pew to pew, some from across a room, others only as far as the wooden dummies they held in their fists.

When he was young he had married a woman called Clarisse who told him that she loved him for who he was, that she wanted to hear only his whisper in her ear, that she was afraid of his dummies, particularly the dog, Munroe. After he married, he had worked as an act on the road with Munroe for two years, playing the carnies, the convention hotels, and the cable comedy shows.

He would shuffle on to the stage, apparently hapless and befuddled. Then he'd sit on a stool, take Munroe out of his box and sit him on his knee and say: "And then, you see, there's the person who I really am," introducing a long-eared, soulful-eyed black dog whose name was Munroe the Hipster, who would take a drag on a joint that he held in his paw and say, "This stuff is hard to get now, man, you got to go all the way to Miami, open up a beachfront window and wait for the hurricanes to blow the seeds in from Cooba."

Audiences loved Munroe.

After a show, Thom would use Munroe to introduce himself to women in the crowd.

"I'm Thom, with a silent *h*, I'm the strong and silent guy behind the dog. It just so happens he knows what goes on in my heart better than anybody."

Women were charmed by the flirtatious Munroe.

Over the two years Munroe seduced several women and Thom bedded them, brief encounters while on the road.

On one such night when he was a little drunk and was about to go into his motel room with a woman, he was sure he heard Munroe, closed inside his carrying case, say: "I hate this fucking coffin."

To make sure he wouldn't be disturbed, Thom had put the case in the clothes closet and shut the door.

"Yes, ma'am," he'd told the woman as he got undressed, "you can't lose what you ain't never had and Munroe never had no cock."

"Gimme some," the woman had said.

"Yes indeed," Thom had said, deeply in love with his life.

Then one day, he had been in off the road and home for three weeks. He was restless. "I am bored out of my mind," he said. His wife, Clarisse, delighted to have him home with her, didn't want to listen to his dummies, let alone talk to them, especially Munroe.

"I want to talk to you. Make love to you and talk to you."

"You don't understand," he said. "When I'm not Munroe, I don't feel free."

"Free at last," she said mockingly, "Oh Lord, free at last."

The next morning, over breakfast, she asked him to be honest, to tell her the truth. She wanted to know if he still loved her and if, by loving her, he didn't feel free, and he, without thinking, blurted out, "No," and he went out into the wide open street feeling that finally, after all his disappointments and tribulations, he was on the loose, and exuberant, full of himself, he laughed at the top of his voice, throwing his laughter straight up into the sky. He waited but it never came back. Not his laughter. Not his voice.

Suddenly, he was just who he was, and he could talk to anybody face to face, easy as asking a man for a streetcar transfer or a ham sandwich, or talking to the sad-faced preachers in his family church about God and why nobody had seen any of God's grace, but then, if he tried to throw his voice, if he sat Munroe on his knee and took him by the throat, Munroe lipped the air but Munroe had nothing to say.

Thom, in a panic, went to his wife.

He knew he had to tell her he was sorry, and so did.

"My whole future life is in your hands," he said. "I was out of my mind. My mind got away from me. I did not know what condition my condition was in."

She touched his cheek.

"Try to forgive me," he said, "and if not, then think of Munroe. He'll have to be silent all his life."

"I don't give two hoots and a holler about Munroe," she said." I care about you. I care only about you, and of course I forgive you."

That night they made furious love.

In the morning, smiling happily, she said: "My God, I thought you were trying to kill me."

"Love'll do that," he said, and went back out on the road, booked to appear with Munroe at a convention of ear, nose and throat specialists.

He shuffled out on to the stage, sat down on his stool, took Munroe out of his box, and with Munroe on his knee, said, "And then, you see, there's the person who I really am . . . ."

At first, it seemed that Munroe could not speak, he gasped for air, and Thom took him hard by the throat.

Thom heard a low growl. Munroe was looking up at him, growling: "Grhhhh, grhhh, grhhh."

And then Munroe said, "I know you, you no good mothafucker . . . you think I'm gonna pimp for you outa my coffin . . . get your ass off this stage . . . get out of my life . . . ."

SHEARING

He had been awake all night, unable to sleep, and when he told her that a man has to have sleep, she told him about sheep, white and black sheep on either side of the border. She told him how black sheep crossed to be with white sheep and turned white, and how white sheep crossed to be with black sheep and turned black. But one day God took away the border, pulling it like a rope through the long grass and all the sheep turned grey as they chased the rope to the end of the world and disappeared into nowhere and that is how God, who has to keep an open eye on things if He is going to be God, stays awake, by counting sheep.

He is still counting sheep because the sheep keep coming.

A DREAMBOOK
OF OUR TIME

I was his priest.

That's what he said, standing in front of my church, St. Peter's Church: "You are *my* priest."

I was not sure by the sound and feel of him that he had ever prayed. He certainly was not seeking forgiveness.

The chill composure in his pale hooded eyes was not the look of a man wanting absolution. Yet he insisted he needed a priest.

"A walk might do us good," I said.

"Stretch the mind," he said.

We went for a stroll along Bloor Street, a clutter of shops on both sides of the street.

When he saw himself in a storefront window, he said, "I have eyes like ghosts."

❊   ❊   ❊

He had large bony hands, he cracked his knuckles as we walked, and he wore a black leather finger-glove on his index finger.

"What's that?" I asked.

"A glove."

"I can see that. What's it for?"

"To keep the finger warm. Safe. My trigger finger."

He touched the glove to his nose.

He had a crooked nose.

Women, he said liked his nose, "lonely women, the kind of women who like to look after things they think are broken," but soon it was clear, after I asked about who his friends were, that there were no women in his life.

Sitting in the Whistling Oyster café, he sang to me:

momma cooked a chicken
she thought he was a duck
she set him on the table
with his legs cocked up

He wore, even while eating in the café, a black borsolino hat. He wore his borsolino night and day.

"A sensible man wears a hat in this country," he said, "and here you are, hatless?"

"Yes."

"That's strange for a priest. They always wear hats in the movies."

"They're old B-movies."

"My father died under his hat, hit by a car. His hat rode on his coffin to the grave. I, too, am to be found under my hat."

❊   ❊   ❊

He had been a soldier in Bosnia, a Blue Beret, a blue-eyed sniper wearing a battle-blue helmet, a peace keeper, a hardened master sergeant who appeared to be modest as a hangman might be modest – Earlie Fires – who, after a 13-month tour of duty, had come home to set up his own one-man company – Earlie Fires, Animal & Pest Control – telling me in his unhurried drawl, "I keep down the vermin."

He also told me, as if he wanted me to understand that he had moments of dark uncertainty, that he sometimes woke in the morning in his bedroom, naked, in a cold sweat, staring at a porcelain cat's face on the wall, the face a clock.

He said the cat had "an evil smile" and a pendulum tail. He could hear the wag of the cat's tail: *te-duh te-duh te-duh* . . . . "You know, like the beating of my heart."

I told him he didn't have an evil smile so his heart could not beat like that.

"Believe me, nothing's what you think it is, my heart beats like that."

❊   ❊   ❊

We sat on the back porch of his house of an early summer evening.

Shad flies clotted the window screens. Hundreds of little silver shrouds. He pointed to two old elms towering over the porch, boastful, like they might be old relatives: "They survived the blight, the Dutch elm disease."

Crows were nested in the high branches, he said, and rats at the roots. He took me by the elbow, about to give me a warning. "Rats don't just run in the slums and on the waterfront but in the fine parts of town, too, fat rats because of good people doing good works," and he chuckled, tweaking my arm, the fatness of the rats a joke on me, on God in His good works and especially on "people of civic goodwill composting garbage heaps in their backyards. Compost, it's fast food, takeout," he laughed, "the heaps are honey pots. Adam rat and his Eve in the Park." There was no compost heap in his yard. But several neighbours had theirs, he said. One was an old man who had apparently survived the death camps.

And the heaps had their rats. To get rid of the rats under his elm trees, Earlie had baited the nest holes with *THRAX* and then he'd waited, cradling his shotgun. As the rats came up for air in twos and threes, he'd sat in a canvas summer deck chair – and he showed me the deck chair that was still out on the lawn – BLAM by five in the afternoon BLAM sixteen rats were dead, the bright red casings of fine-bird shotgun shells scattered in the grass between their bodies.

"I raked up the dead rats, raked them into a heap, drenching them with gas and lit them on fire."

He had fed and stoked a slow-burning fire for more than an hour.

His next door neighbour, and I've since seen him, a dour old man who had been propping up the white heads of peonies in his back garden, "He's an old man who has lived alone beside me for years in his squat little house, he's always out there, puttering around, looking bent and half-bewildered, a mumbler. On that afternoon he had been standing with the wind blowing smoke from my fire across our fence into his garden, into his face, and he stood there, the wind thick with the rancid sweet smell of burning flesh, with ash, until he began turning in circles, beating his breast and pulling his hair, stricken looking, and he started in on this nasal chant: *Yiskaddal veyiskaddash* . . . . And I'm screaming at him, because I can see he's caught up in some kind of chant for the dead, 'You crazy old man, you're crazy, can't you tell the difference?'"

❖   ❖   ❖

The next day as we sat in the Whistling Oyster he said his right eye, what he called his crosshair's eye, hurt. It hurt so much that he put his hand over the eye to hold it in darkness. He wanted me to know he worried about his eyes. "I trust my eyes," he said. "For me, seeing *is* believing. Whatever it is. It *is*. Real, more than real, if it is in my mind's eye. I *am* the sniper."

"You're a sniper?"

"So they say."

"You picked off men?"

He drew little moon circles on his paper napkin:

and humming to himself, *momma cooked a chicken . . .*

When I said I didn't understand what he meant by *momma cooked a chicken with his legs cocked up*, he shrugged, not looking up and replied, "How come she thought he was a duck?" as he drew the **X** of the cross-hairs of his telescopic sight into each circle. Then he told me it was more important for me to know that sometimes, when the pain in his eyes was too much, he played the flute, and then, with a kind of staccato intensity, he told me how he'd come to learn about harmonious musical intervals, how they could be expressed by what he called perfect numerical ratios – and how all phenomena, he said, tapping the table with his leather trigger finger, like I should know that his leather finger was his lethal finger, all the things around us follow the patterns of number, showing me what he meant by drawing it on a napkin, showing me that the sphere, the circle, was of course perfect, but no circle was more completely human (he smiled a wry, surprisingly satisfied smile) than a circle with a crosshair in it, but most beautiful of all – and he took off his hat – was a tetraktys of crosshairs (which I had never heard of),

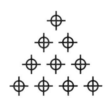

an image, he said, of eternal harmony: and, just as I decided for sure that he hadn't called on me to own up to some terrible crime, but, astonishingly enough, he was outlining for me his idea of what perfection was, he said, "Look, you're a priest, you understand these kind of things," and though I told him right away that nothing is more overrated than the understanding of priests, he carried on breaking it all down for me, telling me how the monad (primordial unity), the dyad (the energy of opposites), the triad (introducing potential), and 4 – the four seasons, the four essential musical intervals – all completed a progression: 1+2+3+4=10, what he called the tetraktys – and it was, he said with a big wide sweep of his arms, the actual numerical model for the kosmos, "the whole damned kosmos" and then he wagged his leather trigger finger at me again – he was now having a very good time with himself, let alone me – it was also, he said, the symbol of the human psyche, "that enraging, frightening, exhilarating space where men have gone in head-first to create some kind of harmony out of the most horrific pain, like the craftsmen for the coliseum in Rome, did I know about them? Artisans, artists who sculpted brass cows big enough to hold a man in their bellies, giving the cows a hinged lid that they opened and then the man, tied in a foetal position, they put him in the belly, the lid was closed, and a fire was built below the brass cow's belly, a fire so they could slowly roast the man inside alive, but what's fascinating," he said, holding me by the wrist, "is that the craftsmen had shaped the mouths of the cows into six small flutes, so that the roaring screams of the dozens of roasting men in the stadium were turned into harmonious song, bursts of light-hearted flute music, pure notes from pure pain, harmonies that filled the air until there was a last drawn-out dying note, a long B-flat."

He smiled, he put on his borsolino.

I thought: *What in the world is going on, where does this man want me to go with him in his mind, and why?* as I put his napkin of crosshaired circles in my pocket.

Then he said: "Ten is the tetraktys, ten is complete fruition, and the question is – can ten killings be a fruition?"

❋   ❋   ❋

We were walking along Bloor Street, a crowded downtown shopping street that was all in sunlight, the men wearing linen jackets, seersucker and white suits, and the women summer floral dresses. I had decided in the morning to not wear my roman collar. He had said immediately as we'd met: "You're not wearing your dog collar."

I said, "No, no because as far as I can figure out you're not wanting me to hear your confession."

"Confession," he snorted, "of course not, the yellow dog's got nothing to confess, I'm a virtuous man."

The yellow dog was new to me but I let it pass as we crossed an intersection against the stoplight. He said he'd been having a hard time with the light, with his eyes, "a lot of pain, ordinary little things, light bulbs going on and off, light stinging off the chrome hubcaps of parked cars, the same kind of sting of light my father showed me one afternoon when I was a child, showing me how to burn ants alive, burn them with a magnifying glass, frying them like he did one-by-one one day until he got bored and poked the nozzle of a can of 2-in-1 lighter fluid into their nest hole, pumping the fluid down, and then he lit it with his Zippo lighter and kept injecting fuel into the fire hole, the mound burning to black sand, burning the bodies to black nubbles" – and then he took me completely by surprise, plunking his borsolino on my head as if we had become secret sharers of his head and all that was in it – "and so you keep this under your hat, now," he said, with mischief in his tone and a menace I'd not yet seen in his eye, "you keep it strictly between us, that's how my father kept me company in the hills outside of Daruvar when I was crawling in the tunnels, the wormholes, we called them, tracking the scent of human fear – I'd always gone into tunnels calmly, my lieutenant saying, '*Sometimes I think someone freeze-dried your nerves,*' going deeper, trying to 'hear' the terror of the killer hiding in there, and I'd always pick a time when I knew I was close to the man, a time to laugh, to snicker, so that the man would know a devil was coming after him, and some started screaming before I ever got to them, boys gone half-mad, and, it was a long time before my own fears at last took me tight by the throat, when I was suddenly dead sure that I was being buried alive, it just heaped up like someone shovelling dirt in my brain that I was being betrayed, maybe by my lieutenant, maybe by some hill country militia thug who was waiting for me to come up out of my hole, waiting for me with his 2-in-1 flame-thrower to burn me alive, to sting me, so that now when I wake up I sometimes wake up with my body sopping wet" – and he reached across and snatched his borsolino from me and jammed it on his head – "and I stand in the corner of my bedroom, naked except for my hat, my wise borsolino, freezing in a night sweat although it's already noon and I'm trying to calm myself, calm down because I've been awake all night, not falling asleep until dawn, the Glock under my pillow, death close to my ear – it's like having crabs on my bones. A clutch. Not panic. A desolation. Something nameless. I empty my mind into a stillness, it's a stillness where singing helps, I found that out while I was crouching down in the stench of a sewage ditch stacked with naked bodies,

> *oh death please sting me,*
> *and take me out of my misery,*

listening to myself – listening since I can't seem to shut myself down, singing and mumbling in my mind, a running, loping, barking dog, that's my mind, running low to the ground, nosing under a log, a gangly yellow dog between the bushes, sniffing at the legs of a little girl who's got freckles and her mother, the two of them straggling along the edge of the road, looking at me, looking at my blue helmet that looks to them like a piece of the blue sky had fallen down between them as they carried on trying to find some small flat stones. Wanting the stones to throw at birds, to kill the birds for food, all the fields stubbled, scorched to stubble, and the trees blackened by fire, the branches settled by small white butterflies, clustered. Shanks of blackened rope. Skull bones tied into the branches of the trees, a bit of blue sky in the bones. Butterflies in the skulls. Each a stillness. Like an empty thought. So empty I needed a priest, I needed a sane priest," and he eased up very close to me, almost cheek by my cheek, whispering, "You see, what was wrong, the whole god damned miserable place was overrun by crazy true believers, priests and mullahs and tribal wackos. Children flensed to the bone by flame-throwers. *Pray for us.* Buckets of men's testicles marinated in kerosene, *Pray for us,* set up as fire pots at night, as landing lights for airplanes. *Pray for us.* Water poured from a tin cup, a final blessing over a bald but heavily bearded old priest propped up on the steps of a monastery. *Pray for us.* His severed hands, severed feet, crossed in his lap. *Pray for us.*

"And all the time I was trying, I was trying as hard as I could to step into the skins of those farmers, to get into the skins of those shopkeepers, those tribal priests, trying to step into their shoes like you're trying to step into mine. That's what I hoped then and I hope now. Trying to make what I'm saying fit. Into something. Any kind of shoe. Anything other than the ineffectual moral arrogance of trying to keep, by the barrel of an empty gun, another man's peace! Which is exactly how I dropped into the line of sight of this warlord who was in charge of the local airstrip. I was out on the tarmac, and there he was, a completely drunk fool crying *fuck fuck fuck fuck fuck,* while I stared at his shoulder insignia. Serbs? *Who were they?* Drunk on malignancy. One saying over and over, 'Flowers, thanks to God are in bloom, no clouds.' Saying that they thought they were going to have to shoot me, a Blue Beret, me with no permission papers where there were no permission papers for anything, so they said they were going to have to shoot me or someone would shoot them, it was necessary since what was necessary is necessary and what is not necessary is not and the crazy warlord nodded, and there I was pointing at my blue helmet, and I kept pointing until I worried they might think I was telling them to shoot me in my head. The drunk militia captain, whose fly was open, told me, 'Mister, please, your helmet, you take it off, yes!' I took it off. 'Put on helmet.' I put it on. Without waiting for his orders, making mock, I took it off, I put it on. 'You play your game,' the furious captain said, 'You wake up dead.' Leaving me with nothing to do but to shrug and say, 'Your fly is open.'

"The captain cracked me across the shoulder with the butt of his AK-47. My blue helmet fell into the mud. 'Now helmet is off. You are lucky. You know why? Why is a very big question,' the captain said. 'Is most important question, Why? Why? Why? Why?' he screamed.

"Then, he smiled. 'Fuck.' He took hold of my hand, the pupil of his eye black to the core, and I looked into that blackness. The cold in his hand a biting cold. A cold that was not the hand of death. It was the cold hand of evil (I look at myself every morning in the mirror, my priest, waiting to see if my eyes have gone black), that was the sign of evil, the blackness of the eyes, that cold hand.

"The captain, he saw an old man sitting by the side of the tarmac, he was sitting there braiding flower stems into a bouquet. He went over and shot the old man. Dead. 'Jesus Christ,' I yelled, 'why did you do that? Why?' He said, 'Exactly. Why? Now you are a philosopher.' Waving his arm, 'You go. Pass freely.' Before I could go he laughed, holding up a weighted sack. 'Here is freedom,' saying he had in the sack the severed head of another warlord. 'No trouble,' he said to the sack, 'you too are free.'

"He bowed to me. Courteous. A fellow soldier. 'Fuck,' I said, taking my helmet off, banging it on the tarmac like I was crazy. 'What a fucking thing to do!' He screamed, 'Fuck you to fucking hell, you do not want to be on bad side with me.' Saluting. He gave me the V for victory sign, telling me, 'Come into my hills I will kill you, too.' I didn't know what to do, you're a priest, what can you do, pray, good works? There was nothing I could do, not then, and not later at a cross-roads when I saw that the head of the other warlord had been taken out of the sack and mounted on a pike, eyes closed, the mouth open and stuffed with oxlips and violets.

"A mouthful of flowers at a crossroads, it sounds, right? A shrine to all those numbed men out there with their need, their inexplicable crazed need for utter cruelty, trying to keep a peace where there was no peace, no battle lines, only skirmishes, fire-fights, and militias made up of stupid ordinary men who were not just killing each other but decapitating, raping, and dismembering – killing off all the enemy's men, the boys, the babies, trying to kill the future, gang-fucking the women and girls to contaminate the bloodlines, to infect the heart, to sow hatred.

"And nobody wanted our Blue Berets, not even the local priest who, totally stripped down, bald-ass naked, bicycled across the airport tarmac to his gutted church, crossing the air to ward off outsiders, to keep us away as, crossing as he past the airport's tiny lounge where an officer who had flown in from Brussels stood and spoke to us, to his Blue Berets: '. . . very well, they choose to suspend the accepted rules for conducting civilized warfare, well, if two play at the game – and that is what they are doing – then those two sides are in violation . . . we abide by rules . . . .'

"'Does that mean we are civilized, sir?'

"'That means we are to enforce the peace by engaging in no retaliatory aggressive action, not against either side, we are to stand between . . . .'

"'Between is where, sir?'

"'Where it has to be.'

"'Could that be anywhere, sir?'

"'Anywhere is where it is.'

"'Yes sir.'"

❋   ❋   ❋

He invited me more and more into his house, his family home, where I realized he talked about all houses the same way. Houses were alive.

"There is life, teeming life," he said, "moving in the cellars, vermin in the walls, from the dust mites we can never see in our beds to the raccoons playing hide-and-seek under the roof."

He had a large bookshelf full of books on woodworms, rodents, centipedes, squirrels, ants, cockroaches, and especially termites – and it was the termites who seemed to fascinate him the most, largely because of the way they built huge insulated housing hives, and – it was like, he said, they had their own military pointmen – they'd send out blind feeders – their own Blue Berets, he called them – who set up forward positions, stone-cold blind but still able to somehow survey the hills.

And then there were the infiltrating carpenter ants, sawing into support beams and the floor scantling, tunnelling and leaving only tiny mounds of superfine sawdust in the corners of a house – apparently he had had his own infestation in his own house, ants nesting in the wood framing above the basement concrete blocks.

He had sprayed all six of his rooms, and the basement, with a chemical called antheletymene, and then he sat down, watching and waiting for them to come out of the walls. He told me that the stillness in which he sat was like his stillness as a sniper: as he'd waited for men to come into his line of sight X, but the antheletymene had turned out to be so strong – so toxic – that his nerves had turned to neon lighting in his brain, he said he could feel his heart ricochet in his rib cage, he must have been taking the chemical in through his pores as if he were an ant himself, and it had brought him to his knees, dancing on his knees in the dark, listening to snakes whistling.

Not long after he told me about the ants, sitting on the porch, he left me to go into the house to get a glass of water, and then I heard him yelling. I found him standing in front of a floor-length mirror in the hall, he was berating himself in the mirror. "But I wasn't yelling at myself," he told me later, "I was yelling at a man who was yelling at me, a man wearing a black borsolino hat, a killer who, as soon as he saw me, he warned me, 'You play your game, you wake up dead,' and because I wanted nothing to do with him I took off my hat, and then put it on, trying to get my hat off and on before he could get his hat off and on, but then, with his sudden sheepish smile, he spread his fingers against his side of the glass, like he wanted our fingertips to meet, to touch, and they almost did, but I pulled back because he had widened his eyes into the kind of eyes that I've seen before, eyes that are haunted, the eyes of a man who has seen oxlips and knows they're a sign of spring in the mouth of a dead man, and I'd no sooner yelled at him, 'You don't scare me,' than you came along, asking me 'Can I help?'"

"Help? What d'you mean *help*?"

＊　　＊　　＊

Earlie gave me a drawing, a drawing he says of the man he saw in the mirror. The man has the nighttime stars of Van Gogh in his eyes, stars crisped to black. I feel the insurgent embrace of suffering in his face, it bleeds to the edges, or perhaps I am wrong. Perhaps it is terror.

❊   ❊   ❊

Listening to snakes whistling was just like being back in the Bibić hills, like I was tracking a palpable scent of human fear, of panic, following my nose, nosing around outside of a small field hospital that the UN had set up close to a gutted farm house and an abandoned orphanage.

A half-track had ground razor wire down into the mud, but after the rains, the wire had risen up. I saw a sliced-off toe, like a white bud about to flower in the mud.

I kept the toe bone as a souvenir, to remember how they grow things there.

And how they have butchered their own lives, and I can see it all but I can't see the answer to the question, the *Why?* Which is why I want you to see the dead carts I've seen upended in the mud. You have to step into my shoe, you have to see that there's still a dead body in one of the carts, the long handles sticking straight up in the air like prongs to a tuning fork (I thought it'd be perfect to find Beethoven between the prongs, brooding on the B-flat harmonies of Moscow on fire), the *clack clack clack* of .50 calibre machine-gun fire up in the hills, *clack clack,* it was like the tapping of a blind man's cane in my brain, the red tracers streaking into the trees clumped

behind the orphanage, the walls that had been buckled
in by mortars, the fruit trees between the orphanage and
the open graves in full bud – white and lemon-yellow
– the same white and lemon-yellow as the gay spring
scarf I saw on a nurse after I walked through a skeletal-
standing doorframe of a house whose front wall had
been blown away, a television still on in the back room,
blaring so loud I'd slid along with my back to a wall to
see who was watching the TV and what I saw was CNN,
this reporter with his wacko angular Australian twang,
his tone of pained urgency as he told me that mass
graves and a concentration camp had been found outside a village just ten minutes away, and I thought, Yes,
because I'd been at that concentration camp ten days
earlier just ten minutes away from where I was now in a
back kitchen where a nurse, a Red Cross band on her
head and a white and lemon-yellow scarf around her
shoulders, a woman who looked to be in her late thirties, was lying on her back on the floor with her legs
spread and angled in the air, angled like you could hang
your washing on her ankles, and between her legs there
was a naked boy – a stripling boy of ten or twelve with
thin wrists and narrow buttocks – a boy, perhaps from
the orphanage – and standing there against the kitchen
wall, cradling my rifle across my chest – I couldn't believe how glistening white her thighs were – and the

boy's body, too – their embrace a stillness in my mind's eye, and I thought – I should report to CNN, I have found a stillness, a toe in bud and a stillness – until she turned her head and, looking sluttishly pleased – she winked at me, as if she was sure I would understand why she was there having a beautiful boy-child fuck her, probably for the first time in his life, down there in the tile and plaster rubble, down there in the reek of cordite.

I went back out into the yard, I wasn't sure whether I was affronted or aroused – into the yard – attached to the field hospital flying the blue flag, to eight cots in a tent, three corpses on the cots, and one squat, heavy-shouldered, iron-haired nurse. Sheets caked with blood covered the sick and injured, not the dead. The corpses were naked (nothing, it seems to me, so conveys the terrible vulnerability and final futility of struggling to live as a flaccid penis lying along the thigh of a dead naked man). Without thinking, I laid my hand on the shoulder of a corpse whose face was yellowish green, his left eye closed below a wound in his forehead, his right eye open, staring straight up. I shut my left eye and stared down, sniper to sniper, I thought, as the nurse, who had liverish bags under her eyes, said, "You want to do something good . . . ?"

"Sure," I said, "I'm a good man."

"You find the one with the hammer, you kill him."

She turned to a man lying on a cot. His wound over his collarbone was running pus. She applied a poultice that smelled, after she had unwrapped it, of sulphur.

It looked like a goat's or sheep's liver.

"Jesus Christ, what's that?"

"Is poultice," the nurse said. "Do your own business."

"I'm going," I said, "to check out the orphanage."

"The hammer. Not forget. Do something good."

So, my priest, like I set out to find you in your church, I set out to look for the hammer, in the orphanage to do something good out there among the fruit trees, some burned to a bone crisp, others loaded with white and lemon-yellow bud and I thought – though I didn't smoke – I had this crazy thought that in the movie about my life this would be the time, the place, to stop and smoke a cigarette. And then, in the movie this would be the moment, with me standing there relaxed and guileless, I'd get shot by an unseen marksman, shot as I took my first deep satisfying drag, and in my memory's eye that shot taught me to always keep an unseen marksman in my mind's eye, sniper to sniper.

In the orphanage, in the dining hall, under the wall icons of two saints with fire-eyes inlaid in silver – on the other side of several rows of polished oak dining-hall tables – I found a dead woman lying on the blood-stained linoleum floor, a young naked woman, spread-eagled. Nailed alive to the linoleum, naked and nailed down, at her hands and feet, with long roofer's nails, nailed and raped.

Until she was dead.

Her bones were still in her skin . . . but not because she hadn't tried to get out of her skin, her skin . . . her back was still arched up off the floor, surging in a last attempt to get loose of the nails . . . her mouth wide open, her perfect white teeth, eyes bulged out of their sockets. An empty champagne bottle by her foot, the room stifling. Shit and rotting flesh. Flies. No white butterflies. Wobbling fluorescent green flies. Hundreds of them. I wanted to get my own bones out of my own body, sickened, in a fury at the futility of young bodies piling up till the trenches overflowed. The rats feeding. Then, a pause in the clock happens. And a little cuckoo bird sings . . . . Time-out. Peace. There's a prize. Except, there's always a rat in the clock, there is always a rat in the clock behind the bird – behind the door – (the bird thinks he has found his escape hatch, so dumb in his memory that he thinks this every hour on the hour) – and the bird sits out there and he sings, but always a spring goes CLICK and the pause is done even before the mustard gas and the smoke and ash from the furnaces settle and the bird gets snatched back into the clock and the door slams shut, CLACK – and it is Hello Pol Pot *Pray for us*, Hello Putin *Pray for us*, Hello Stalin *Pray for us*, Hello Pinochet *Pray for us*, Hello Mao *Pray for us*, Hello Hitler *Pray for us*, Hello to all the Doctor Strangeloves – and then, sometimes – except for the moving hands on the clock, there is that pause, that calm, there is a lull in which, as soldiers, as Blue Berets, as peacekeepers, we sit tall in our tanks at a crossroads, models of rectitude, but soon the rats begin to feed, they rape, they behead, they are the generals, the police, the bishops, the mullahs, the rebbes, the tribal militias . . . And so, what was I to do, what good was to be done for my iron-haired nurse? What was required? What is required as the door slams shut, CLACK, and it all begins again, the eruptions begin again, the buboes, as the unbelievable becomes all too believable, when a woman disembowels a man and tries to stuff his live baby son into his stomach. I was outraged, I, who can sit in utter stillness for three or four hours – letting all the anxiety drain out of me, absolutely relaxed, not limp – relaxed into focus, complete focus, coiled for action in my mind's eye, trusting my eyes since *seeing* is believing, since I *am* the sniper, coiled yet at ease, as if I felt the moment before and the moment after come at the same time – a moment so satisfying – and so prolonged in its tension within that stillness, in that O, the X of the crosshairs, that once or twice I almost did not pull the trigger, wanting to hold on to the feeling, but as I told you, my priest, the decision I made – not just to disobey my orders – but to kill certain men, and one woman, was taken in all intellectual awareness, a decision to act, and by completing the act, completing its virtue, my own act of virtuous violence.

"Ah yes," you said to me, my priest, "Aquinas, a matter of intellectual virtue independent of morality."

Perfect.

I was not wrong to have sought you out. You got the point exactly. Which is why I have let you look into my eyes, I've let you see my ghosts, feeling no rectitude, as I rehearse in my mind how I hunted down, on separate occasions, split off from my squad, those I intended to kill. So let us make no mistake, my priest, I knew exactly what I was doing . . . *I have not only seen evil but more important, I understand that I have seen evil,* I have seen it in an offering of oxlips in a dead mouth at an empty crossroads. It's not the thought that counts, it's acting on the thought. I tracked nine men and a woman who had become monsters of evil. Monsters. Not machine-gun jockeys. But monsters who believed they were safe, safe to go back up into their hills, confident that those of us who were there to keep a peace would not only never kill them but would protect them from each other. But not me. I drew each one of them into my crosshairs, into the circle of my gun sight, with a silencer and from a distance, so that no one knew where the shot had come from. I shot them dead in their shoes. I eradicated evil.

✛ – the Hammer, seated on a kitchen chair, bearded, lifted his hand, held a slice of bread warm from his wife's oven, then slumped over his kitchen table, bleeding from the mouth into a soup bowl

✛ ✛ – the airport warlord, sitting cross-legged on the stone step to his village well, petting a dog, his string bag full of tomatoes, and then his body jerks back, the dog licks blood from his blown-open throat

✛ ✛ ✛ – a man, an ex-doctor, who was known as the Stitcher because he stitched up the mouths of people he was going to kill, once sewing a live mouse into the mouth of an old woman, driving her insane

✛ ✛ ✛ ✛ – a professor, offering a book to his wife as I'd seen him offer the hand he'd severed from a six-year-old girl to a guard dog on a chain

✛ ✛ ✛ ✛ ✛ – the woman who disembowelled a father so that she could then try to bury alive his baby son inside his stomach, the father, of course, left still alive for this

✢ ✢ ✢ ✢ ✢ ✢ – a tinsmith at his work table wearing a leather apron, making a breadbox, who had used his soldering irons to burn out the eyes of a mullah, shot from behind, blowing out forehead bone and eyes

✢ ✢ ✢ ✢ ✢ ✢ ✢ – the man who'd sowed a playing field outside the front door of a kindergarten with land mines and then had hurried all the children out to die as they tried to run and dance through the mines, shot clean through the heart as he sat with his own children

✢ ✢ ✢ ✢ ✢ ✢ ✢ ✢ – a woodsman who was a militia gunner who cleaved a woman's skull from crown to chin with a power saw, gutting it and then placing her hands, severed at the wrist, in the skull, shot between the eyes as he took outdoor Communion

✢ ✢ ✢ ✢ ✢ ✢ ✢ ✢ ✢ – the gas station attendant who, as a captain, drowned men by forcing a nozzle into their throats and then firing them up as human bombs, (my only near-miss), his jaw blown away

✢ ✢ ✢ ✢ ✢ ✢ ✢ ✢ ✢ ✢ – and finally the commandant who drowned a prisoner every day in the camp cess-pool, shot as he bathed in a mountain pool, shot in the shoulders so that he could not swim to stop himself from slowly sinking

Ten times, my priest. I killed, my priest, ten people.

And my killing them was an act as impersonal as a hangman is probably impersonal, unlike the killing of someone like my mother or father – or you – would be personal, but then of course, I can't kill my mother – I never knew my mother – and I can't kill my father because he is already dead. He died just before I went into the army, though he still moves around in the house, I know him by his step, I hear the creaking of the floors, his step slow and hesitant, his presence like an incursion, a shadow moving in and then moving out of me along with my other ghosts, those ten, who inhabit me the way vermin inhabit a house, they leave behind a superfine trail of sorrow, a sorrow that heaps up and sits heavy on my mind, especially in the morning when I find myself not refreshed by sleep but overcome at the beginning of the day by an unfathomable ache, by what I believe is not despair, something beyond Why?

"What is that?" said the priest.

It is a sense of desolation.

It is a state. It is virtue in desolation.

Consider that, my priest. Could you live there in that state as I do? Could you live there alone?

"No, I could not, I'm a priest."

※　　※　　※

Again, we were on the back porch. Earlie was wearing his black borsolino and he had bought me a borsolino as a gift, so there we were, two men sitting side-by-side on a back porch, sitting under two old elm trees wearing black hats. And he was playing his flute. A simple melody, a pure pleasure to hear, a song he'd heard in the hills outside Daruvar.

I asked him if I could give him a gift, if I could make a blessing, a sign of the cross over him?

He said, "No, not over me. If you want to bless the garden, be my guest."

I did.

Then, putting down the flute and after a silence, he said: "My father told me that memories are a ladder and if you walk back and forth under a bad memory you get bad luck. Some men, he said, live under a ladder all their lives. I killed those ten people, I make no bones about it. I am not sorry. I live under the ladder of their deaths. I regret nothing.

"Every day I draw a deep breath, take off my hat, and look into it.

My beautiful borsolino hat.

I bring the hat up to my face.

Eyes open I cover my face with darkness.

I smell my smell.

'Yes, that's me,' I say, as I say to you now.

Then I go to the kitchen,

momma cooked a chicken

she thought he was a duck
set him on the table
with his legs cocked up
And I eat ice from the refrigerator.
Ice is good for the soul, it brings down the swelling."

MERMAID

He woke up hearing the ocean. He closed his eyes as if he were still asleep and listened because he was nowhere near an ocean. He had been born in a concentration camp and he had survived the camp and made a life for himself selling insurance and now he was sixty-years old and having never been to an ocean he was in bed with a woman who thought she was old because she was thirty-eight and he thought she was young because she was thirty-eight. It was her bed, the pillows were of soft down.

"Do you hear the ocean?" he asked. He had never slept all night in anyone else's bed.

She opened an eye. Her left eye. It was a pale ice blue, it was a blue clock, he thought.

He couldn't remember her having blue eyes.

"Yes," she said. "I love swimming in the ocean."

"You do?"

"Yes."

He was worried that if she opened her other eye it would be blue, too.

"I was sure you had brown eyes," he said.

"Because I'm a mermaid," she said. "All mermaids have brown eyes."

She laughed. Her teeth were very white and the tip of her tongue between her teeth was pink. She drew his head down to her belly, between her thighs. He took a deep breath.

He could smell the ocean.

He tasted the ocean.

"Only great men have ever slept with a mermaid," she said and opened her other eye.

It was blue.

"You're no mermaid," he said.

"Welcome to the real world," she said.

"No, no," he said.

He was still strong, lean and muscular. He made a fist and showed her the inside of his forearm, a tattoo.

It was a mermaid.

"You've got a mermaid tattoo on your arm," she said.

"No, look very hard," he said, and he drew her head down to his arm.

She said his skin smelled like smoke, she had smelled it all night. He said, "No, just look, look hard."

She looked and at last she said, "Numbers. There's numbers inside the mermaid."

He said, "Yes, they disappeared in my little mermaid."

"Why'd you do that?" she asked as she lay back in her soft bed.

She looked almost unbearably young to him.

"Because I am alive and she is now my real world. She has brown eyes and those others who gave me the numbers are dead and they had blue eyes," and he leaned over her and lightly kissed her eyes closed and said, "Now we make love again."

CROSS-PURPOSES

The high winds that whip themselves through the valley in the winter bring on a cold that will break a man's eyes, but those selfsame winds come to a stillness in the summer. Without those winds there is a blazing heat and no rain and with no rain the farms suffer from what Ernie Lidle, neighbour to Elmer Lidge, calls the blight of infection, and he is right to call it a blight because the whole of the valley, even the willow scrub which grows like a weed, seemed in this summer to take on an illness, the field crops almost overnight turning a withering yellow. The earth began to parch at the roots and if a man put his ear tight to the ground he could hear that parching going on, like the breath was being slowly forced out of the roots.

It sounded like the whispering of ghosts, the ghosts of the wolves who'd been in the valley in the wintertime. Ghosts that would spook a body, turn a person strange. Strange enough for Lidle to get himself his old army .303 one night and fire off four rounds at ghosts, he said, were playing hopscotch down his lane. Then, of course, he laughed. He said, "Actually, to say they were playing hopscotch is going a touch too far; they were just there, hanging loose in the stillness, and anyway, I like talking to ghosts, they talk to me about God."

But the whispering really did spook Elmer Lidge – a man who was prone to praying even on sunny days – the ghosts not only spooked Lidge but his cattle beasts, too. And his pigs. There were several pig barns and sheds in the valley. It was the pigs not ghosts that put a spook on Lidle's mind. Pigs were said to be smarter than horses but, to put it plain, they are cannibals and if there's no rain and the pigs are lying thirsty in their pens, they'll rip the living throats out of each other. Screaming like they do, almost human, it goes like knives up into your brain, right behind your eyes and turns you half crazy.

Lidle, inclined to hope, though squinty-eyed and seeming suspicious, he told Lidge that he had consulted the regular almanacs and prophecies and he had been encouraged to "fear for the best," the best being an unusual increase of summer winds. But instead of the best, he stood side-by-side with Lidge and watched the strong early July rains come cold-cocked to a halt right at the mouth of the valley, watched how they just died down, stopping, Lidle said, like it was the hand of God Himself who – for reasons of His own whim or for spite – had stilled the winds. Lidle said sourly, "You know what I say. I say life is like that."

Lidge, a stern ex-special-forces sergeant, who had battle patches from Cyprus and Kosovo, but possessing that strange giddy goodwill of the reborn believer about him, was always keeping one eye peeled for signification and sign, "whispers from the Holy Ghost," he called them, like one day when Lidle was talking to him by the door to the Lidge drive shed, Lidge got excited, saying that the whole countryside was sick, that illness was in the air, that he'd seen a bird, a red-wing blackbird walking backwards, "And birds don't back up, they can't back up," he'd cried, "so something terrible is gonna happen upon us."

He'd got down on his knees. He'd prayed all that afternoon. He'd prayed hard, which didn't surprise Lidle because he knew that Lidge had a clockwork habit of going into his house every noon to have lunch with his unmarried sister who kept house for him, and he would look up as he went in, saying to the crucifix nailed over his front door, "O Lord, I wait upon Thee and Thy grace." Lidle, his mouth dry, would squeeze his eyes shut and say to Lidge, "There is a God, I still believe that, but there is no grace." Lidle had talked like that to

Lidge, flat-toned, not looking to pick an argument, but sternly true to the fact of what he thought and felt ever since his wife had died, dying a terrible death from a cancer that had incubated as an infection in a tooth of her lower jaw. She had died clenching a prayer cloth between her teeth that she'd got by mail order from the Reverend Hagee of Texas. "The infection started as an ingrown canine tooth," Lidle'd said to Lidge, "and then the cancer ate her up and Jesus, like He had a cancer Himself, didn't say a word." It was five o'clock in the afternoon.

Lidle had the county newspaper folded under his arm. Lidge rolled a cigarette, drawing the paper across the tip of his tongue.

"They say the ice packs are all melting."

"They say a lot of things."

"That they do."

"But I've a mind we know what's what."

"We do. And what we don't know, too."

"True."

By mid-July, it had gone rainless for three weeks. The farmers in the valley, whether they were watching birds walk backwards or not, knew that they had to get their first crop of hay cut and, as the red clay fissured and cracked, they had to make sure that their pigs were well-watered and kept apart. The cry of a thirsty pig would thin your heart. Lidge, who wasn't just thin but strangely narrow across the shoulders, narrow in the hips, laughed and said that "it kept him thin keeping his pigs fat." His head was narrow, too, between the ears, like he'd come out of the womb and got squeezed coming down the canal. The cry of the pigs upset him and he said to Lidle that he'd found his cattle beasts acting strange, too, standing upright in his fields all night – like they were afraid to lie down – and they had begun to groan at night, and he said, turning sideways and looking over his shoulder, as if he was looking for the worst, confiding in Lidle, "I think the ghosts of them wolves has got inside the cattle beasts."

"Wolves've got their night life," Lidle said, laughing.

Then, with no warning whatsoever, the sky took on a yellow cast, a yellow that became slashed with grey, and finally it turned pitch black. The rains poured down. "That's the grace of God," Lidge cried, tears welling in his eyes as the heavy rain came down to pour straight through the valley, pelting the crops, a steady soaking of the fields that turned to a punishing hail. Then it stopped, like the downpour had been a taunt. After a pause, it rained again, a fine rain, every second day, for a week.

"The gentle and gentler rains of the forgiving Jesus," Lidge said,

And one day Lidle and Lidge stood feeling giddy in a sun shower that Lidle said was more like seeing a shower of sun, and Lidge's sister, Annie, said that she was going to make a jubilation lunch for the monthly meeting of those valley farmers and some of the boys from up the valley, she was going to make it in the Legion Hall, and soon, with the showers falling steadily it was so lush in the valley that there was sun moss in the roof troughs and the fields were ready to ripen, especially the rapeseed, a blazing yellow instead of the sickliness of wasting away. "That yellow," Lidge said, his fist balled with excitement, "that yellow is the yellow of God's eye, the nurturing eye."

Lidle said, "The only yellow eye I've ever seen was the yellow eye of a pariah dog."

Lidge, thin as he was, liked to tell Lidle – with aggressive buoyant goodwill – that he was "fat in his heart for Jesus," and that's exactly what he had said as he promised Lidle that he was going to give Jesus praise for the rains. "Fat praise from a thin man." He leaned back and laughed. He sang. He knew only the beginnings of songs. He stood at the head of his lane that cornered two concession roads and a long grassy knoll,

> *see the pyramids along the Nile*
> *see the jungle when it's wet with rain . . .*

never wanting to be hasty, yet stubborn in his resolve as he went to work on the knoll with a post-hole rotator. "Going down," he cried, and then, after he had dug a deep hole, he took off in a wobbly trot down the lane and disappeared into his barn.

Lidle, having been troubled by a dream of a man with no hands, went by the Lidge house the next day. He spoke to Annie. "I dreamed I was touched by a man who has no hands." She wagged her head. "I dream about that man all the time." In her voice there was a tone of sadness as she added quietly, "In the land of Edom . . . ." And he said, "What about Edom?" unable to remember where it was, reminded that there was something acetylene in her dank faith, having none of her brother's wondering-eyed expectancy: "They both got good teeth and a hard bite, except he smiles," Lidle once said. "You can see him coming. With her you never know."

But Lidle didn't see Lidge for three days. He had disappeared into the barn. Lidle heard him sawing and then *silence* and banging and then *silence* and one night he heard high-pitched squealing from behind the door.

Then, on a Friday, Lidge came out of his barn. He was dragging a heavy cross. On the cross, nailed to it, was what Lidle – in school – had called a stick body, but this body was big as life, with a head on it. Lidle stood aghast. Lidge had covered the body with a fresh pig skin, a pig he'd butchered, a skin that he'd blowtorched the hair off of and scoured and scraped to bring it close to a human pink, fleshly, with an open gash where the genitals should have been.

With gouged-out eye sockets and a crudely painted face with a tin nose on the head, and because it had a trimmed horse's tail for hair, it appeared to Lidle to be a kind of ghost of the real Jesus nailed to the cross, which Lidge then boosted on his shoulder and tipped into the post-hole, bolstering it upright against the blue sky with stones piled at the base. Lidle, coming up close, caught between bemusement and wariness, said, "Do you think, I mean, do you think I could have a word with Him, like He might know something new to say."

"Jesus is the answer," Lidge said.

"I don't like to ask any more questions than I have to."

"Yes," Lidge said, backing away, "yes, yes, Jesus."

"What I'd like to know," Lidle said, cocking his head up to the cross – but then he let go of his question, let go of the silence, and he stood listening to Lidge who was bent over praying in an abide of poplars a short distance from the cross, suddenly envious of Lidge yet resentful. The trees in the abide were thick with birds that had been brought on by the rain – bobolinks and red-wing blackbirds – and Lidge's nasal melancholy whine rose up through the chattering birds: "The Holy Ghost, hear His summoning call." Before the afternoon was out, other farmers and their wives had come to kneel or slouch about the foot of the cross, mumbling prayers.

However, as the week passed it slowly dawned on Lidle – not on Lidge – that despite their prayers, despite the mortification and thanksgiving, the valley air had come to a stillness again, the rains had stopped, the heat had suddenly risen and reached a dry burning of close to 100 degrees. "If that was the yellow eye of God," Lidle said, "then God is wanting to put a hurt on us." Lidle said he could hear, during the day, the dry crackle of crops as they began to parch and shrivel, and at night, the cattle beasts moaned, and by the time a week had passed the soil itself was hard-packed and caked and the sun moss in the troughs had turned to a slime and then to a crust.

Lidle found two dead birds on his porch stairs.

He resented the dead birds.

It seemed to him that the closer the crops got to drying up and dying in the fields, the more the body on the cross came alive, with a freshness and thriving pink in the flesh, crucified but flush for all who stopped by the concession road to see.

Annie, tall and thin-lipped, insisted – offering to swear an oath in front of Lidle – that she had seen the slash of His mouth turn to a smile, a fleeting smile bestowed on her, she said, a smile of His satisfaction.

The next day, as Lidge knelt in prayer, Lidle stood behind him, his pale, pale blue eyes unblinking, cradling a rifle in the crook of his left arm, demanding of the crucified body, "Say something!"

When he heard no word he said:

"Thought so," and tapped a cigarette out of a soft-pack, snapped a wooden match one-handed with his thumb, and lit the cigarette, and said, "You better say something," as he blew smoke through his nostrils, and then, before Lidge and Annie, he lifted his rifle and shot Jesus.

One shot. Clean.

Annie collapsed and tried to curl herself around the foot of the cross.

Lidle said, "That's that. No more games."

Lidge stepped back, and stepped back again.

He held up his hands, saying he'd heard Jesus on the cross give out a deep sigh. He said that Jesus was still sighing, still alive.

Lidle said, "Not likely," and went home.

Within an hour a fresh wind had come up, a strong fresh wind, and then, hard on the wind there was rain.

By the end of the day, farmers stood in the rain together singing. Lidge sang,

I saw the harbor lights

and clapped Lidle on the shoulder. People spoke of Lidle
as a man who had dared to do the right thing. To celebrate the rains, several women cooked and served a supper at the Legion Hall. Only Lidge and his sister stayed
away, sending a handwritten message, a quotation from
the Book of Amos. Nobody could make out what it said.
It had got smeared by the rain. The crops came back to
life, "with a vengeance," one of the farm women said,
even the fields that had never been known to be green,
on the high slopes of the valley, up to the line of scrub
pine, a line that was a dark necklace around the valley.

Lidge began to wear black, a black shirt, black hat,
black boots, and every night in the rain, wearing a black
slicker, he kept vigil at the foot of his cross. At first –
until a week or more had passed – no one paid attention
to him, but then he started whispering behind his hand
to neighbours that Jesus was coming back to life, too,
that he could now see new life in His eyes, life in the
pink colouring of His skin. Lidle came by to smoke a
cigarette with Lidge and he stood beside him in a drizzle on the knoll.

"Them ice packs must really be melting for there to
be all this rain," Lidle said.

"I wouldn't know about that."

"Well actually I wouldn't know either."

"I know the heart of Our Lord has melted in His mercy."

Lidge had to admit that Jesus did look to have life in Him and it was not long before the rapturously inclined believers in the valley – standing at the foot of the cross – began to speak smilingly of the End Days – of the rising up of the saints – an evaporation out of this world, body intact, into the embrace of God. They began to hold ecstatic prayer meetings in the shadow of the cross – "This new sign," as Lidge hollered out, "of the resurrection. He who became as all men are, and being as all men are, He was humbler yet than any man, accepting death, death on a cross."

His voice carried across the knoll and on the wind, but after he spoke a third time, the wind became dry. A woman was washing clothes bare-headed under a burning sun. Her husband warned her not to waste water. She waved her white kerchief gaily in the dry wind, and following on the wind, there was no rain, there were no sun showers.

The sun was relentless. The crops withered, the clapboard siding on farmhouses and barns shrank. Lidle stood on the road in the dust and screamed, "Goddam, goddam. He don't say a word." The crucifix over Lidge's door fell to his porch floor – too heavy; its long shingling nails had come loose in the shrunken wood. He didn't notice, nor did any of the others in the Lidge prayer circle notice that their cattle beasts were staggering in broken circles at night and were collapsed with their tongues lolling during the day. Worse, there was a rancid sweet stench coming from the pig barns and coming from the cross. Sickened by the stench, Lidle said, "This is abominable, cleanliness being next to Godliness, we're pigs living in our own shit."

Lanky, all elbows and knees, he strode down the concession road repeating in a low menacing voice the Lord's name. He looked neither to the right nor to the left, nor to Lidge who was among his followers gathered in the abide of poplars for an evening of Bible study. Lidge, helped by Annie, was handing out scissored squares of sailcloth that he had blessed. Lidle showed them no sign, except that he took a prayer cloth from Annie and stroked it down the length of his rifle barrel, stroking and bringing the barrel to a sheen. Then, he lifted his rifle, looked up to the face on the cross, paused – alone in his pocket of silence – and then he fired four rounds into Jesus.

"This time You're dead for keeps," he said. He sloped his rifle in the crook of his arm as if he had been shooting grouse. A wild-eyed charging Lidge, followed by Annie and the other worshippers, punched and kicked Lidle. They booted him until blood came out of his mouth and nose. Annie bit his finger. She bit the tip of his trigger finger off and spat it at him. They tied him with ropes, hand and foot, and hauled him down the lane, dragging his heels in the dust. They kept him overnight in the pig barn. Annie lit a bonfire in the lane and several of the women said they saw ghosts, and heard them howling. "Maybe they're angels," a woman said. "No, they're wolves." Annie said. "But it's not winter yet," the woman said, as they all kept vigil outside the barn until morning when Lidle, half-crazed in his eyes, mumbling, "The blood . . . listen to the blood," was brought out bound by his arms and belly and shins to a cross. Another rotator hole had been dug. "Going down," Lidge cried and his neighbours tipped Lidle's cross into its hole. Lidle, an eye swollen shut, hung face-to-face with Jesus, who had given up His pinkness, as if He had given up the ghost. The skin had tightened on His body. It had turned stiff, it had cracked, turned dark brown.

A shower of rain fell for a few minutes. Then it stopped.

There was nothing. They waited. A yellowing, a feverish infection, spread through the farms in the valley. It spread quickly. Pigs became so crazed they had to be shot. Lidge said he heard dry thunder. "Bone dry," he cried. He read verses from the Gospel of Mark, saying the words of Mark were the right words to read to Lidle because there is no resurrection at the end of the Book of Mark, just an empty tomb and bewildered women. Two men driving a pickup truck and wearing hoods arrived at the knoll on the third morning. They called out: "You, Ernie Lidle, killer of Christ." Blistered by the sun, Lidle lifted his head. He looked at Jesus. "You should have said something," he whispered. And then: "I'd like to be home."

"Hell, don't he know that home is yesterday?" one of the men said from under his black hood.

On the count of three they shot Lidle. He made no sound, he bled very little. A light breeze rose up as they cut his ropes and handed his body down and then there was even more of a breeze, a breeze with a surprising tang on it. "The winter's on us," one of the men said as they buried him in an unmarked hole behind the Lidge pig barn. Lidge took down Jesus and wrapped Him in one of his own bedsheets and kept Him in the Lidge house on an old horsehair sofa until they could lay out His torso in a glass case, a case that Lidge had made for the Legion Hall.

COMMUNION

The old man had a long blade nose and a hunch to his shoulders, as if he were huddled against a heavy sorrow. Head down, whenever he came on Sunday to Our Lady of Perpetual Help, he was late for Mass, coming in after the sermon, standing at the back of the church, stern and discomfited, by the ninth station where Veronica wipes the face of Jesus.

Another latecomer caught the coldness in those eyes as he passed him.

He withdrew his wrist with its blue tattooed numbers, and his hand, into the sleeve of his coat and then, as if he were an elderly war amputee, he extended the empty end of the sleeve to the other latecomer. "You can't know what you can't see," he whispered. The other latecomer stepped away and dipped two fingers into the holy water piscina by the door and made a small cross on his forehead to protect himself against what he could not see.

At the ringing of the bells, at the changing of the bread and wine into the Body and Blood, the old man got into the line going up the centre aisle so that he could stand in front of the priest, put out his hand, and take Communion. He held the wafer in his open palm, stared at the white O as it lay across his lifeline, felt it on his tongue, and let it dissolve a little. He wanted to bite into it, to swallow this God, and he did.

HE DREAMED

He dreamed that he was a liar. He dreamed that he lied about everything, even trivialities. When he was asked why he lied he said, "I've this dream, that I'm a story-teller."

He dreamed that he was living alone in a small house close to a river and railroad tracks, close to where he had heard trains hoot through the valley.

He dreamed that his army uniform had been stolen by a scarecrow and that his house had a chicken coop just like all the other houses in the valley, a coop at the back of vegetable gardens. He kept six hens and an old rooster. The hens were scrawny, the rooster was so old that it often forgot to crow in the morning, and even on the best of mornings the hens laid only a handful of eggs.

He dreamed that he had written a little story about his First Communion and he was feeling so alone and sorry for himself that he read the story to the hens.

He dreamed that the story might cause them to lay more eggs.

His hens clucked and went to sleep.

In the morning, the old rooster stood staring at the dirt and a lone egg. He dreamed of guinea cocks, he dreamed of owning his own fighting rooster.

Then, one afternoon at the local market, he lied to the butcher and said he hadn't eaten for three days. The butcher, feeling sorry for him, gave him a laying hen because it had a broken wing. On the way home he felt around the broken bone of the wing and, in among the underfeathers, he found a single gold feather.

He dreamed that the gold feather was a sign.

At dawn, there was only one egg under the broken wing of the new hen but he was astonished, and then overjoyed. The eggshell was gold.

The next morning, he dreamed of another gold egg.

And a gold egg every morning after that, breaking the eggs over a pan, making himself an omelette, gathering up the gold shells. After two weeks, he dreamed of opening an account – currency for gold – with a warlord back in the wartorn hills, where he also went to a breeder of game cocks and bought the most vile-tempered rooster in the breeding shed.

He dreamed that the bird was so vicious it pecked out the eyes of the cocks it killed.

With his cockfight winnings and cash from the gold, he went to town where he met a boy dressed as a girl, Slavenka, in a hotel close to the train station.

He bought Slavenka red shoes and red wine, and in the morning, when they woke in the hotel room, Slavenka said that listening to the trains in the night had led to a dream of water and the sun.

He said, "I know how to read dreams."

He went to his house, left enough feed for two weeks in the coop, chained the killer rooster to a wall, and then he and the boy, who was wearing red shoes, travelled to an island in the sun called Krk. They made love and he lied and said he loved her. She lied and said she loved him. On the third day they were yelling at the top of their voices about money and Slavenka said they could be free only if he never went back to the house in the valley. "You're rich, the rich don't need a home country."

Slavenka stole his money from his pockets, and left the red shoes under the bed. He came back to his house dreaming of a coop full of gold eggs, and a riled-up rooster ready to kill.

The rooster couldn't fight, he had hurt his beak by pecking the chain. There was nothing to eat. The hen had sat on all her gold eggs, hatching them. He dreamed of gathering up the broken shells but he did not go to see the warlord. There might be snipers in the woods.

He dreamed about swarming clusters of hatchlings, whose feathers shone with the glitter of gold lamé, who screeched as they spun in distempered circles, who seemed to grow older than he was and then scurried past his legs and disappeared into the long grass.

He dreamed that he heard the killer rooster, father of the hatchlings, growl.

He dreamed that he heard a train in the distance and the sound of hatchlings coming back down out of the hills, crashing through the woods. He dreamed that something was required, that the leader of the hatchlings would make demands, so he cut off the head of the fighting cock, the killer rooster.

He heard screeching in the woods.

"You don't scare me," he lied. He held the headless bird in the air, placating he didn't know who, and then he packed the gold shells in his satchel of stories about himself.

"I'll catch a train for the border tonight."

The hatchlings, who had broken into several tribal militias, and who were now so huge and so vicious that they tore at each other's throats, came striding at him out of the long grass.

"So," he said, looking the biggest hatchling, the old storyteller, in the eye, "You are the truth. I die a happy man."

ACKNOWLEDGEMENTS

In **BETWEEN TRAINS** the old storyteller says that an older storyteller had, in Paris, told him a one-line story: that elder among older storytellers was W. Somerset Maugham.

PIANO PLAY was published in *Exile The Literary Quarterly*, and in *Raise You Ten: Essays and Encounters, 1964–2004, Volume Two.*

A PROMISE OF RAIN was published in *Hogg, The Seven Last Words.*

PAUL VALÉRY'S SHOE was published in *Exile The Literary Quarterly* and in *Writing Life: Celebrated Canadian and International Authors on Writing and Life.*

SHEARING was published in *Hogg, The Seven Last Words*, and in *Raise You Five: Essays and Encounters, 1964–2004, Volume One.*

MERMAID was published in *Exile The Literary Quarterly.*

The story **HE DREAMED** has its root in a folk tale or story I read long ago, about a hen that had a broken wing, a gold feather, and not too friendly hatchlings. I would be pleased to hear if anyone knows the original tale.

I wish to dedicate two stories
to *Kim McArthur*
my publisher extraordinaire:
"Dog Days of Love" and "Without Shame"

Special thanks to *Marilyn Di Florio*
for her long-time commitment and assistance

True gratitude for the trust I have in my night riders:
Seán Virgo and David Sobelman.